RIVERS EDGE

A RIVER WINERY NOVEL

JEN TALTY

"*Deadly Secrets* is the best of romance and suspense in one hot read!" *NYT Bestselling Author Jennifer Probst*

"A charming setting and a steamy couple heat up the pages in a suspenseful story I couldn't put down!" *NY Times and USA today Bestselling Author Donna Grant*

"Jen Talty's books will grab your attention and pull you into a world of relatable characters, strong personalities, humor, and believable sto-rylines. You'll laugh, you'll cry, and you'll rush to get the next book she releases!" Natalie Ann USA Today Bestselling Author

"I positively loved *In Two Weeks*, and highly recommend it. The writing is wonderful, the story is fantastic, and the characters will keep you coming back for more. I can't wait to get my hands on future installments of the NYS Troopers series." *Long and Short Reviews*

"*In Two Weeks* hooks the reader from page one. This is a fast paced story where the development of the romance grabs you emotionally and the suspense keeps you sitting on the edge of your chair. Great characters, great writing, and a believable plot that can be a warning to all of us." *Desiree Holt, USA Today Bestseller*

"*Dark Water* delivers an engaging portrait of wounded hearts as the memorable characters take you on a healing journey of love. A mysterious death brings danger and intrigue into the drama, while sultry passions brew into a believable plot that melts the reader's heart. Jen Talty pens an entertaining romance that grips the heart as the colorful and dangerous story unfolds into a chilling ending." *Night Owl Reviews*

"This is not the typical love story, nor is it the typical mystery. The characters are well rounded and interesting." *You Gotta Read Reviews*

"*Murder in Paradise Bay* is a fast-paced romantic thriller with plenty of twists and turns to keep you guessing until the end. You won't want to miss this one..." *USA Today bestselling author Janice Maynard*

HAVE WE GOT A STORY FOR YOU!

Dear Readers:

Welcome to Candlewood Falls!

Each Candlewood Falls story stands alone. However, the end of one story doesn't mean the end of your favorite characters. They can show up in any Candlewood Falls book at any time.

Candlewood Falls is a unique world of connected stories by different authors whose characters, business, and events appear in each others' stories.

Think of Candlewood Falls as a literary soap opera.

Be sure to check out the the other authors and discover which other books include your favorite characters.

Happy reading!

Stacey Wilk & K.M Fawcett & Jen Talty

This is a work of fiction. Names, characters, places, and incidents are the product of the author's imagination or are used fictitiously. Any resemblance to actual persons, living or dead, or actual events or locales is entirely coincidental.

RIVERS EDGE

Copyright © 2021 by Jen Talty

Printed in the USA

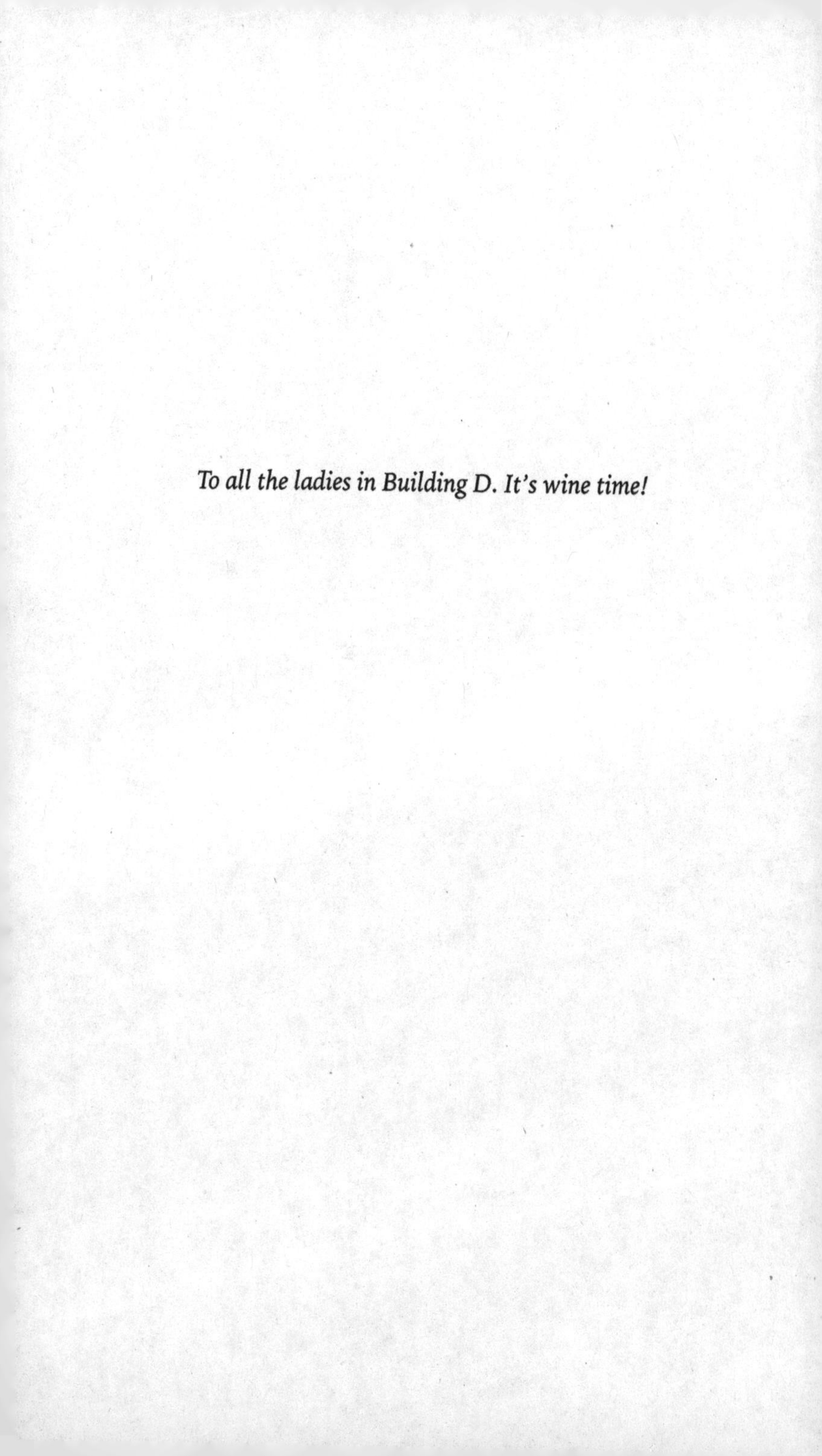

To all the ladies in Building D. It's wine time!

1

MALBEC

Malbec River set his cell, screen up, on the counter. While it was only seven in the morning where he lived, it was ten in Candlewood Falls, New Jersey. If it were really important, his mother wouldn't bother to leave a message. She'd hang up and send a text demanding that he answer the phone when she called in about five minutes.

If she had the patience to wait that long.

Otherwise, she would move on to one of her other six children she'd successfully pushed away.

Of course, everything these days seemed painfully important in Weezer River's life. Just because Malbec was the oldest didn't mean it was his job to talk his mom off the ledge every single time something happened at the winery that she didn't like.

Which seemed to be an everyday occurrence, and

why Malbec wanted her to really consider doing the one thing she'd swore she'd never do.

He pulled down an oversized coffee mug and set it under the Keurig.

His mother's name flashed across the screen.

Mother: *I know you're awake. If you're not alone, good for you, but this is important. Pick up the damn phone.*

He rolled his eyes as he stirred in some cream and sugar. He didn't know what was worse: His mom's constant questions about his love life or the lack thereof.

Or the fact that she was still trying to get him to move from Napa Valley—where he had a job with one of the best wineries in the country—to go work for the failing family business that he'd been trying to get her to sell.

The phone buzzed just as he brought the mug to his lips, and the coffee burned the roof of his mouth. He tapped the screen. "Good morning, Mother."

"Don't *Mother* me," she said. "I hate that."

"Would you rather I call you Weezer?"

She let out an audible sigh. "It's just that when you say it that way, it makes me think you're not happy to hear from me."

He stepped out onto the patio and inhaled the fresh scent of grapes. He chuckled because it reminded him of home.

There was plenty to miss about Candlewood Falls, but being Weezer River's son in a small town had been something he ran from the second he graduated high school. Between his parents' divorce—which was only on paper and living space since they couldn't seem to keep their hands off each other—and his mother's manipulative ways and inability to let anyone other than her make decisions regarding the winery, it kept him from going back.

Besides, no place in the country was better for him to do what he loved more than anything than Napa.

He could cultivate grapes and make some of the most delicious wines that money could buy.

If nothing else, his mom was proud of his talents, even if she never once hinted that she cared. Deep down, he knew his mother puffed out her chest every time she talked about Malbec and his accomplishments. It was impossible for her not to boast about her children.

"I still have no idea where I got that nickname from."

Malbec burst out laughing. Cordy Wilde had given his mother the name when she was a teenager. Over the years, the story had changed and grown, but it started when his mother snuck out one night to meet his father and Cordy caught them in somewhat of a compromising position and the nickname had something to do with the noises Cordy heard.

It's also rumored that Malbec was conceived that night.

But that might be a bit of a tall tale.

"I'm so glad I can amuse you, child."

"You always do." He set his mug on the table and pulled out a chair. The morning sun hit his face, and he blinked. If he were being honest, he missed his family —all of them, including his mother.

Especially his mom.

As difficult as that was to admit.

"What is so important that you had to interrupt morning sex? I hope it doesn't have anything to do with that story about my ex-girlfriend."

"Good Lord. No. And please don't ever mention that woman in my presence again. But the first sentence got me all excited. Do you have a girl with you? Who is she? Is she in the wine business? Are you going to bring her home? More importantly, does that mean you're coming home for good?"

He shook his head. He should know better than to get *the* Weezer going. "I was joking, Ma."

"I know. You do this to me every time." She laughed. "But you're not getting any younger, you know. I had four kids by the time I was your age."

"And you and Dad were driving each other so crazy, you ended up divorced."

"We still had three more kids after that."

"Yes. I'm well aware of the twins and my baby sister." His family had sure given the town something to talk about. He waved to his neighbor as he strolled to the mailbox to get his paper. Malbec had to admit, he'd grown tired of living in a one-bedroom apartment by himself. At thirty-eight years old, he had to agree with his mother.

It was time to start a family.

Only he had no prospects, and according to his father, he was too damn picky. However, if he listened to his sister, Zinfandel, he was waiting for his mother to actually find him his perfect match.

Now that was hysterical.

Most people might say he was the spitting image of his dad, but it was the personality traits he'd inherited from his mother that seemed to be a turn-off when it came to long-haul relationships.

Or maybe it was just his mom.

The last girlfriend he'd brought home had made it perfectly clear that she did not care for his mother and wouldn't have anything to do with her or New Jersey. Malbec might only go home a few times a year, and his mom was a lot of things, but he still loved her. And Candlewood Falls would always be a huge part of what made him tick. So, any woman he planned on going the long haul with had to appreciate everyone in his family—and Candlewood Falls.

"I have to admit, I'm always hoping there's a girl." His mother's voice sounded more disappointed than anything else.

"You and me both," he said. "Now, what can I do for you this morning?"

"I need you to come home."

"Why?" He raised his mug to his lips. "As in right now? Is everyone okay?"

Outside of Thanksgiving, Easter, and Christmas—which Malbec always returned for—his mom and dad constantly looked for reasons to pull him back. He'd told his dad that he'd do it on two conditions.

That was if he got to run the winery the way he saw fit, and if his mom filled him on the big secret.

That was something Weezer River would never do. Ever.

"I have a buyer for The River Winery."

He spit out his coffee. "Crap," he mumbled. "Are you shitting me?" He wiped his mouth with his hand. He wanted to ask his mother about the secret his grandfather had spoken of on his deathbed, but he didn't want to start an argument about something his mom had made perfectly clear she would never fill him in on.

Not even if Malbec did the one thing his mother wanted more than anything in the world and came home to run the winery. So, what the hell was the point in bringing it up?

"Nope. She'll be here in a couple of days. I'm hoping we can close the deal, but I need your help."

"When did you put it on the market?" Sucking in a sharp breath, he tapped his chest. Weezer River was not the kind of woman who asked anyone for help. While the family business did well enough, for Malbec, it could do better. And for him to put his name on a bottle of wine, it had to be the best. His mother was too stubborn to change her ways and get with the times.

Or, more importantly, listen to her eldest son, who happened to be an expert in the field.

"I didn't. She came to me. And she's the perfect person since none of my kids wants to run the winery." His mother's voice was laced with the same tinge of frustration she always had when the topic came up.

The problem wasn't that Malbec didn't want it; he just wanted it on his terms. And he knew his mother would stand over him with a watchful eye as if he were a toddler.

"And you're seriously considering selling it?" he asked. Part of him was waiting for the other shoe to drop. His mother was a kind and loving mom, but as a person and a businesswoman, she could be ruthless. And this was one of those situations where if he didn't hold onto his hat, she'd take it.

"I'm pushing sixty. I want to enjoy my golden years."

Another chuckle tickled his throat. His mom was not only young, but she would also probably outlive them all. "What is it that you need from me?" He swallowed the thick lump in his throat that told him not to trust his mom and this information. But if there was anything he needed to know, his family would let him know. He quickly pulled up his text messages.

Nothing from his siblings or his father.

This must really be on the up and up. No way could his mother have a buyer and keep that juicy piece of intel from her husband or her other children—or anyone else in the town.

Holy shit. Malbec was getting his wish, and he wasn't really sure how he felt about that.

"I want to know if she's capable. And since you're better at this than I am…"

He coughed. He should have known. "What are you really up to?" Only on rare occasions did his mother hand out compliments. Usually, it was reserved for when she talked to someone else or wanted something.

"Malbec. I'm tired. I've been doing this for as long as I can remember, and when Grandpa died and left it all to me at the ripe old age of nineteen, I thought I was on top of the world. Now, it sucks the life out of me. And if you've made a good name for yourself out there in Napa, I accept that."

He checked the time. "Did you go hang out with the gossip ladies this morning and drink a ton of mimosas?"

"Seriously, Malbec. Put a fork in me, I'm done. Now, can you come home and help me? Your father is useless."

"I am not." His father's voice boomed in the background.

Malbec shook his head. "Hey, Dad. It would have been nice to know that I was speaking with both of you."

"I literally just walked into the winery and overheard that last part," his father said.

"So, is Mom really selling? And are you okay with that?" Malbec stood and took his mug back into the kitchen. If his father had been part of any of those discussions, then it had to be true.

"Do I really need to explain how this works to you, again? Your mother gets whatever she wants."

Oh, boy. This would be a long rant.

It always was, and there was no point in trying to cut his father off at the pass. When Carter River got started on a story, there was no stopping him.

"She didn't want to get married at first when we had you, so we didn't. When she got pregnant with Chablis, she went out and found the ring she wanted. When she wanted a divorce and to sleep in different houses, well, that was simple enough. She's not an easy woman to live with, but she *is* an easy one to love."

Malbec wanted to argue that point, but he knew better.

More importantly, he really wanted to repeat the question. However, he figured that would be a bad idea. In his father's mind, he'd answered it.

"I do have some vacation time I can use, but I can't be there until next weekend." Malbec rinsed his cup and set it in the dishwasher. "I probably won't be able to stay for more than a week."

"That should do it," his mother agreed. "Thank you."

"You're welcome."

"I've got to run," his mom said. "I love you. Send me your flight information."

"Love you both." He tapped the screen and set his cell on the counter. "Holy shit," he whispered. When he was a small child, he'd dreamed about running The River Winery. But when he went off to college, between his mother's manipulations and spending some time working at a world-class vineyard in Napa Valley, it'd sealed his fate.

However, it would be nice for his folks if he spent a little time in Candlewood Falls. Maybe Caleb would show up.

That made Malbec laugh. The last time he'd seen Caleb, he'd been arrested for a crime he didn't commit and then basically chased out of town, never to return.

Malbec would text him anyway.

Just in case.

Weezer

Weezer River couldn't help but smile, even though her heart pounded so fast in her chest she thought she might actually have a heart attack.

For real this time.

"I can't believe I'm going along with this bullshit."

Carter leaned against the counter in the winery's gift shop, folded his muscular arms, and shook his head.

With his broad frame, silver hair, ice-blue eyes, and even his disapproving glare, he was still the sexiest man Weezer had ever met—she just couldn't live with him.

Not on a regular basis anyway.

But there were times she wished she hadn't ended the marriage. That had been a mistake. Hell, she'd questioned everything she'd done since finding out the truth about the winery.

"Don't you want our firstborn back where he belongs?" She quickly finished the list for the morning staff and set her pen on the counter. She picked up the so-called family crest. She often wondered if there was a real family heirloom out there somewhere and not some fake one that her grandfather had handed down through the generations.

Her father had sworn to her that his father and his father's father had no idea that it was a fake, but a small part of Weezer didn't believe that. Especially when she'd found out the truth about how The River Winery had landed in her grandfather's hands to begin with.

"You all but ran him out."

"I did not. Why do you always put that on me? It's not like you didn't put it in his head that his talents might be better used somewhere else." Only she *did* chase her son away, as she did all her kids, and she knew it. But she'd never admit to it. Not yet. Maybe once Malbec was home. With a wife. And had given her a grandkid or two.

Okay. Just home. She could live with that.

If he came back, the rest would follow. Though the twins weren't that far away, and Zinfandel lived in town. The rest all lived within an hour's drive. But still.

The point was to get her family back together after she'd all but torn them apart once. She found out about her grandfather's secret. To this day, it still haunted her. The only person she'd ever confided in was Carter. And if anyone else ever found out, the fine people of Candlewood Falls wouldn't simply point and whisper, "*Watch out. There's Weezer.*" No. It would be the kind of scandal that shook the town worse than when Caleb had gone to jail for something he didn't do.

Poor boy.

Always misunderstood.

Just like Weezer.

And, of course, Alpacino. She'd have to go visit him shortly. He'd appreciate what she'd done. Chewpacha on the other hand? Well, that alpaca didn't get shit. It wasn't that he was dumb, he just wasn't as bright as Alpacino.

"That's not what happened, and you know it." Carter closed the gap and wrapped his strong arms around her body.

She wanted to push him away, but she couldn't. He always offered her comfort, even when she was pissed as hell at him. "You did suggest that he learn from other vineyards."

"Of course, I did." Carter kissed the top of her forehead. "That way, he could bring back everything he learned. But you were being too stubborn to see that." He brushed her hair from her face. "Your father had just died, and that secret spooked you to the point where it even scared me."

She rested her hands on Carter's shoulders. "I've always scared you."

He smiled, which made his blue eyes sparkle like bright aquamarines. "You know I'll support you in trying to mend our family. But it's hard when you refuse to clue me in until after you've done something, and then it's too late to talk you out of it or even fix the damage you might have done without even knowing it."

One of the things she loved about Carter was that he didn't push her too hard. Maybe he should. It had been during that dark time after her father died where they'd almost ended things between them for good.

"I'll tell him the truth about not selling the winery when he gets here."

"And what about Eliza Jane? What will you tell her?"

"It won't matter because Malbec will already know the truth." She rose on tiptoe. "She'll stay on, and I can wrong a right."

"It's not going to be that simple."

She smiled. Sometimes, Carter needed to be more positive. "Hopefully, they'll fall in love, blending the two families forever, and make us grandparents."

"Oh, good Lord, woman." Carter brushed his lips over her mouth. "Will you ever stop meddling?"

"That's like asking the apple orchard to cut down their apple trees." She gave her husband—technically *ex*-husband—a squeeze. "I've got a lot of things to do in the next few days. Are you still planning to be here when Eliza Jane arrives?"

He nodded. "But I want you to promise me that other than being honest and making the proper introductions, you won't push our son onto this young woman. We need her to stay on board, no matter what happens. Especially when you tell her the truth about who she is and what this land means to her."

"I love you with all I am, but I will not make that promise. Especially about telling her anything unless she and Malbec become a thing."

2

———

ELIZA JANE

Of all the places Eliza Jane Blue thought she'd find herself living and making wine, small-town New Jersey wasn't one of them.

As she passed the Candlewood Falls town sign, she felt a smile tug at her lips. Colorful leaves filled the tall trees. She'd had no idea that autumn had begun to settle in the northeast as early as the beginning of September. Having lived in the southwest for most of her life, she'd only seen pictures, and they hadn't done the array of lavish colors justice. She nearly missed the turn to the winery as she stared at the beauty.

She blinked as she pulled into the parking lot. The run-down building wasn't exactly what she'd expected based on the beautiful pictures Weezer River had sent. However, from what Eliza Jane had read, she knew she was faced with a few challenges.

One of which was the fact that Weezer's son had

15

abandoned ship. And whenever someone asked Malbec why, he gracefully avoided the question. His mother never took interviews. However, Eliza Jane could read between the lines. Besides, Malbec had made quite a name for himself in Napa Valley, working with one of the finest wineries and vineyards in the entire country. He didn't have his own label, but he *was* considered one of the top viticulturists and vintners in the country.

Eliza Jane wanted her name on a bottle, and The River Winery could give her just that—especially with Malbec living his best life on the other coast. Not only that, but since none of the children wanted anything to do with the business, there was a very real chance that Eliza Jane could someday own stock in the winery if she played her cards right.

It was something they could discuss something that Weezer had given a lot of thought to, and they would discuss when the first year was up.

Eliza found a quaint coffee shop in the middle of town and decided to stop. She could seriously use some caffeine. She stood in line and glanced at the special board.

"You want the pumpkin spice and the apple fritter," the woman behind her said. "It's the best in all of New Jersey."

"Thanks," Eliza Jane said.

"No problem. Are you new in town?"

"Yes. I start work today at The River Winery."

The woman's eyes went wide. "Really? What will you be doing there?"

"I'm the new viticulturist and vintner. I'll also be managing some of the operations."

"Oh. That must have Malbec's panties in a big old wad," the woman said.

Eliza Jane knew all too well about Malbec and his history with his family. And she worried about that very thing. Still, she wasn't about to discuss that with a stranger. "It's not going to be a problem."

"I hope for your sake it won't be."

"I'm Eliza Jane. And you are?"

The woman glanced around. "I used to know the family. It's probably better if you don't know who I am." She pointed. "You're up."

"Oh. Thanks." Eliza Jane ordered exactly what the woman had recommended and then turned to thank her, but she was nowhere to be found. Eliza Jane handed her credit card to the young girl at the counter. "Did you see who was standing behind me?"

"No. I'm sorry. I didn't."

"Okay. Thanks." Eliza Jane took her coffee and treat and headed back to her car. She plugged in the winery's address and drove out of town. A few minutes later, she pulled down a long, windy drive.

She parked her small SUV in a guest spot and shut off the engine. Reaching across the vehicle, she opened the glove box and pulled out the picture of her great-grandfather. She ran her fingers across the image. "This is for you and Grandpa and Daddy," she whispered as she thumbed the sign that read *The River's Edge Winery*. She glanced up and looked around. The scenery was similar but different. Besides, the River family had founded The River Winery, and it had been in their family for generations. The only thing it had in common with her great-grandfather was the name.

She wished she'd known where her great-grandfather's winery had been located. According to her father, he'd only owned it for a year, and it was more than a sore subject in the family. No one ever talked about it, and if they did, her grandfather shut them down quickly.

She stuffed the picture back into the glove box and stepped from her vehicle. A cool breeze rustled her long, red-brown hair. She quickly snagged a ponytail holder from the many she kept on her wrist and wrangled her mane into a messy bun on top of her head. She inhaled sharply and smiled as the crisp scent of various grapes assaulted her nose.

Leaving her last job had been a big risk. She'd told herself that she had to stop meandering from one vineyard to the next. This last place had given her stability, and while she'd never achieve her ultimate goal of having her own line and a stake in the winery itself, she'd known that she could have been successful there.

But she wouldn't have been satisfied.

She glanced at the sky and whispered an apology to her grandfather. Selling the family's small, novelty winemaking business probably wasn't what he'd had in mind when he told her to go out in the world and put her name on a label. And, frankly, she could have probably done that right there in her father and grandpa's shop.

But after her father passed, she knew that it was time to step out into the world and make a name for herself—one that her father and grandfather could be proud of.

It would take a few years to establish herself at The River Winery, and even longer to create a label of her own wines. But Weezer had told her that it was time to change things up, and after doing a little research on Weezer's history, and that of her winery and family, Eliza found that Weezer rarely went back on her word.

And if she did, it was because she had been backed into a corner, it had to do with her kids, or someone had crossed her.

Everyone warned Eliza Jane not to get on Weezer's bad side. Said that if she ever did, she might as well consider any contract she signed null and void.

A tall, older gentleman with graying hair strolled across the parking lot, a slight limp to his steps. He wore a pair of dark jeans and a dark, long-sleeved shirt with *The River Winery* logo on the chest.

"You must be Eliza Jane," he said as he waved.

That had to be Carter. At least, she hoped.

"I am." She reached into her car and pulled out her oversized purse, flinging it over her shoulder. Butterflies filled her stomach. She'd heard some wild stories about Weezer, her husband, and their family. However, everyone she spoke to in the business had told her that they were good people. Stubborn and often did things their own way, which was why the company wasn't doing as well as it could have been. However, despite all that, she'd also been told that Weezer had single-handedly sabotaged her business all in the name of forcing her son to return.

That seemed to have backfired. Now, Weezer was ready to move forward on a different path—one that included Eliza Jane.

"It's a pleasure. My name is Carter River." He stretched out his arm.

She took his hand in a firm shake.

"Weezer should be back any moment. We had a minor problem with the fence between the alpaca farm and the river's edge, where she planted some new grapevines. One of the alpacas keeps escaping, and he has a special affinity for the new grape." Carter leaned in. "My ex-wife says she dislikes the alpacas, especially Alpacino, but I think she wants to run off with him."

"I'm not sure I even know what an alpaca is."

"They are kind of like llamas, but not really. Honestly, I think Weezer's the one who keeps breaking the fence and letting the alpacas onto our land, because it started happening before I entered the picture. Only, Alpacino is the only one that really ventures in. It's as if the rest of them are truly terrified of her—like everyone else in this town."

"May I ask why?"

Carter waved his hand toward the main double doors. "That depends on whether you are asking about why everyone is afraid of Weezer, or why Alpacino is the only damn alpaca that comes on our land."

"I'll bite. Both." The entryway was a solid oak barn door. She glanced around at the rustic building as she stepped into the lobby, impressed by the detail that had gone into the woodwork. It needed work, but the bones were more than there.

"She doesn't feed the other alpacas, so they don't venture that far down the property line. They don't have any reason to."

"That's mean," Eliza Jane said. "Now, why is everyone so scared of Weezer? She seems nice enough."

"Are you telling me you didn't do your research into our background?" he asked with a chuckle.

"Of course, I did. But I want to hear it from you."

Carter smiled. "My wife's bark is a hell of a lot worse than her bite, but I still wouldn't go getting on her bad side. She knows how to hold a grudge, that's for damn sure. And during this first year, you're going to want to make sure you do things her way and only her way. Otherwise, you might find that my ex-wife is less generous than originally stated."

"You've referred to Weezer as your wife and also as

your ex-wife. Why is that?" Eliza Jane had a few big personality pitfalls—the worst being her curiosity. She shouldn't be asking such personal questions within five minutes of meeting someone, but she just couldn't resist. This family was so fascinating, and their personal history was even richer.

"Technically, we're divorced. And we don't live together. But we are most definitely in love and a couple." He shrugged. "From the outside looking in, it's complicated. But it's really not. And for us, it works."

"No judgment from me." Eliza meandered into the main tasting room. Again, it had a rustic farm feel. She wanted to make a few changes, but she'd wait a week before compiling a report and having a sit-down with Weezer. And Eliza Jane would have to be mindful not to step on Weezer's toes. Right now, her job wasn't to tell Weezer what to do, but to make suggestions for improvements. "My parents divorced when I was young. I haven't seen my mother in years. I have no idea where she is."

"I'm sorry." Carter leaned against the back wall. "That's very sad."

"I don't know any different." Eliza Jane had no emotional connection to her mom. While she could pull up a few memories, she really didn't have any fond ones—or negative ones for that matter—to feel bad about. Her mother had been there; and then one day, she wasn't.

It was that simple.

"I should warn that Weezer will tell you she's going to let you run the show, but she won't really let you. She's tried to let go of the reins in the past, but it's impossible for her to do so. Not completely, anyway. Your best bet is to take things very slowly and follow her lead. Bringing in a manager who isn't family is a new concept for Weezer, and it hasn't been easy."

"She warned me. As did many in the business. Actually, to be honest, some recommended I not take this job." She swallowed the words. She shouldn't have said that, but what was done, was done. She couldn't take it back now. "But since we're on the subject..." She stood in the middle of the room and stared at Carter. "What about your eldest son, Malbec? What are the chances he wants to come back and run this place? I know how talented he is, and I can't imagine he wants a stranger in here."

"He's not coming back," Carter said pretty quickly. "At one point, he wanted to manage this place. It was his dream until he landed in Napa Valley. Greener pastures called, and he's quite content where he is. That's all Weezer and I want for our kids—for them to be happy."

"I have to admit, when I worked in Napa, I loved it. But when Weezer offered me a line of my own in the future and a stake in the winery, I couldn't turn that down."

"That's only after we see how this works." He held

up his hand. "I don't mean to say or act as if we won't follow through, but we have to make sure this is a good fit for all of us."

"I understand," she said with a nod.

"We haven't created a new wine since our youngest was born. I'm sure Weezer told you that you can't mess with those seven signature blends."

She opened her mouth just as the main doors flew open.

"So sorry I'm late." A woman wearing a pair of oversized ripped jeans, combat boots, and a camouflage shirt barreled into the room. Dirt covered her, but oddly, her graying, shoulder-length hair was perfectly styled, and it appeared as if she'd just put on a fresh coat of makeup. "Jenna had an opening, and I took it."

"Who's Jenna?" Eliza Jane asked.

"She owns the salon in town, and she's the best. I set you up with an appointment this week."

Eliza Jane felt her eyes go wide. She'd been warned that Weezer not only liked to be in control at the winery, but she also tended to micromanage all her employees—both on and off the job. That was, in part, why she'd gone through a few winemakers in the last five years when it'd just been Weezer and her husband —or *ex*-husband. Whatever.

That was confusing as hell.

"That really wasn't necessary," Eliza Jane said as she twisted a strand of hair that had a few split ends.

"It's my treat. I like doing things for all my new

employees. And I also got you a tarot card reading in a couple of weeks."

Carter covered his mouth and laughed. "What on earth did you want or need from Faith that required you to purchase a reading? You think all that psychic crap is for the birds."

Weezer rolled her eyes. "I do, but I also think it's important for our new viticulturist and vintner to meet all the business owners in town. Which is also why she's going to man our booth at the orchard this year."

"Now that's a good idea," Carter said as he squeezed Weezer's shoulder. "I do have my other job to attend to."

"Other job?" Eliza Jane felt as if she were watching a tennis match; only she didn't know who was winning, much less who she was rooting for.

"My husband is the best lawyer in town."

"Oh, really? My grandfather went to law school. What do you specialize in?" Eliza Jane asked. Her grandfather had no passion for the law. He loved making wine, even though his father's reputation in the business had made it difficult. He and Eliza Jane's father had a little local shop where they helped people make and bottle specialty wines. It was a fun business, and it kept their family history of winemaking going.

Eliza Jane wanted to carry on her great-grandfather's passion for grapes, even though the old coot had managed to gamble away nearly everything he'd ever owned. Still, she'd heard stories that he had a real talent and taste for wine.

"Whatever you need. Except for divorces." Carter laughed. "I'll see you ladies later."

"Let's take a walk." Weezer led Eliza Jane behind the counter, into the back room, and out into the vast vineyard.

She sucked in a deep breath and closed her eyes for about ten seconds. She could smell the earthy aroma mixed with the tang of the grapes. They were ripe and ready to be plucked from the vines and processed. Of course, these wouldn't be ready for drinking for a few years, but she could tell this would be a good vintage, and she was excited to get working.

She blinked. Her entire professional life had been building to this moment. It was her time to shine. Her moment to make history.

"We just started harvesting, so this is the perfect time for you to learn our process for our specialty wines."

"You're just making the seven right now, correct?" Eliza Jane had purchased all seven wines from two different years. While they were good, they should be better.

She planned on being the person who put The River Winery back on the map as one of the best in the entire country—small vineyard or not.

Weezer nodded. "I'll be honest, I always thought my eldest boy would come home and run things, but he's made it clear that he's happy in Napa Valley, and the vineyard he works for *does* treat him well." She lowered her chin. "Though, no other vineyard will ever put his name on a bottle because of this." She waved her hand. "But he says he's just fine with that, and I believe him."

Eliza Jane couldn't help it. She let out a big sigh of relief, but she still had a few nerves rattling around in her gut. "Malbec has no problem with me being here?"

"You know my son?" Weezer jerked her head. "This is a small industry."

"No. But he is well known," she admitted. "And I did my homework.

"Of course, you did." Weezer continued strolling down the path. "I wish Malbec wanted more to do with The River Winery, but he wants the big corporation with all the prestige that comes with it. And I can't give that to him."

"What about your other children?"

"The twins and our youngest sell our wine across the country. Without Malbec, they aren't interested in taking over management. Our other kids all have different careers and haven't the knowledge." Weezer had a slight tremble in her voice when she spoke about her kids, but her words took on a harsh edge whenever she mentioned Malbec.

Eliza Jane was more than curious. She had to bite the inside of her lip to keep from asking more probing questions. As a small child, her father used to tug at her hair and call her Curious George every time she became too inquisitive.

"You will get the opportunity to meet the whole clan next weekend." Weezer beamed with pride. "Even Malbec is taking some time off work to grace us with his presence."

Eliza Jane coughed and swallowed her breath. She figured she'd end up meeting the man, the legend, but she'd thought it might happen over Thanksgiving or Christmas. Not this soon.

She worried he might see her as a threat.

Which, in a way, she was. But only if he wanted her to be.

She wiggled her fingers as she followed Weezer through the rows of fine grapes. While the buildings, property, and presentation of the winery needed a shit ton of work, the vineyards themselves were in tiptop shape.

That would make her job a lot easier when it came to making quality wine.

Now, all she had to do was restore beauty to the winery and its reputation for being one of the best places in all of New Jersey.

"You never really answered my question about how Malbec feels about me taking over as manager."

"As long as I don't sell the place, he's okay," Weezer said.

"I don't mean to sound rude or anything,"—her heart lurched to the back of her throat—"and I don't mean to ask such a personal and perhaps insensitive question, but what will happen when you're no longer—?"

"You want to know what happens when I'm dead, don't you?"

Eliza Jane's father was likely rolling over in his grave and whispering that this was none of Eliza Jane's business. Only it was. This was her future. Her last chance to make the kind of mark in the wine world that she'd always dreamed of doing, and she wouldn't let anyone take it from her.

Not even the owners' son.

"Yes," she admitted.

"That is a good question, and something we need to sit down and discuss with Malbec."

Eliza Jane's heart dropped like a cement brick, plummeting to the depths of the deepest sea.

"Don't worry. If you work out, as stipulated in your contract, I want to make sure that you will stay on if my family continues running the winery."

The agreement was for one year. If Eliza Jane proved her worth, they'd offer her a more permanent role— and her own line. If not, they'd send her packing.

She believed in herself so much that she knew the latter wouldn't happen.

"And if they don't?"

"Then perhaps your time here will give you an option to buy. But that's putting the cart before the horse now, isn't it?" Weezer looped her arm through

Eliza Jane's and guided her through the maze of grapevines and toward the far side of the vineyard, where a small river wove its way through the property. "How about I show you where you will be living?" She pointed to a small building. "I've had it cleaned and made sure you have a new mattress and sofa since the other one was about twenty years old. It's basically a studio, but you'll have everything you need."

"I'm sure it will be fine. And I like the idea of living where I can see the vineyard."

"A small access road runs on the other side where you can drive your car. I'm sorry there is no carport, but Carter and the twins should be able to build you one before the snow gets too bad."

"I would appreciate that." While this small cottage on the river's edge was going to be where she lay her head for the next year, she was going to make Candlewood Falls her home.

Permanently.

3

MALBEC

Malbec decided to take the red eye a day early. In part because his mother always enjoyed it when he surprised her with an early visit, but also because he wanted to have a conversation with his father about the sale of the family winery. He was positive that his dad wouldn't let the vineyard go without getting top dollar. Malbec's heart grew heavy as he pulled down the access road leading to the cottage by the river.

He'd lived there a couple of summers when he'd come home from college, and every time he came back for a visit since. His mother always tried to get him to stay with her, but she often didn't understand personal space. And if he stayed with his father, his mom would end up crashing there. At least at the cottage, he'd have a little privacy.

"What the hell?" he whispered as he parked next to

a small SUV. Perhaps his mother was having it cleaned for his arrival. That made sense.

He yanked his suitcase from the trunk of the rental before locking it. He pulled his keys from his computer backpack and strolled across the brick pathway. A million bittersweet memories flooded his brain. He loved this piece of land. It was a part of him and no matter where he was in the world, something always reminded him of home.

He opened the front door and set his bags by the small table. "Nice," he whispered. His mother had finally gone and splurged on a new sofa. He furrowed his brow. The bed wasn't made, and the closet door was open, with clothes hanging inside—women's clothing.

That didn't make any sense.

The sound of water rattling the pipes tickled his ears.

He eased toward the bathroom door and pounded on it twice. "Who's in there?"

The sound of a female screaming filled the room. The click of the lock echoed. "I have a gun, and I'm calling the police."

"I think I'm the one who should be dialing 9-1-1 since my family owns this place. Now, who the hell are you, and why are you in my mother's cottage?"

"I work here," the woman behind the door said. "I'm the new winemaker and manager. Weezer is letting me rent the cottage."

"My mom would never, in a million years, let anyone besides herself—or maybe me—make River Wine," he mumbled. His mother had sworn to him that she'd sell the place before she let that happen, and since none of his siblings had neither the knowledge nor the desire, that was the only option.

Maybe it was time the family let go and let someone else make this place theirs.

"Please, open this door. I'm not going to hurt you or anything. I just want to know who you are and why you're staying in the cottage that is normally reserved for family."

"I will do no such thing. You'd better leave now, or you will have to answer to the police."

"That's not going to be a problem. As I said, my family owns the winery." He scratched his head, contemplating his next move. He really hadn't wanted to tell his mother that he was in Candlewood Falls yet, but perhaps he should give her a shout. He pulled his cell from his back pocket and let out a long breath. This conversation would suck. It was one thing to show up on his mother's doorstep with a bouquet and a smile. But to call her? He rubbed his ear. That would surely piss her off, and that was the last thing he needed. "Hey, Siri. Call Mother."

She answered on the second ring. "Hello, Malbec. Are you all packed?"

"I'm that and more," he said. "I need to ask you

something, and I want you to promise me you won't start yelling or hang up on me."

"You know I can't do that."

He pinched the bridge of his nose. There was no point in putting off the inevitable. The longer he waited, the worse her response would be. "Who is staying at the cottage and why?"

"The only way you'd know that is if you were already here. And if that's the case, I'm not sure whether I'm thrilled to death or so angry I want to put you six feet under in an unmarked grave where no one can find the body."

He chuckled. His mother always spoke her mind and said things that no one else would dare. Once, when he was about seventeen and stole a bottle of wine to impress some girl, his mother had commented about how she should kill him, only that would land her in jail. She'd said that in front of half the town, who'd all let out a collective gasp. As if his mom would ever lay a hand on *any* of her kids. She was actually a very kind and loving woman, but the town never really saw that side of her. Only her family did.

"Mom, please just answer my question. I'm standing in the cottage, and some girl has locked herself in the bathroom. She threatened to call the police, and she says she's the new winemaker and manager. That makes no sense when you're about to sell the winery."

The door flew open, and out stepped the most

gorgeous woman Malbec had ever laid eyes on. Her long, auburn brown hair cascaded over her shoulders, and she wore only a sports bra and a pair of spandex workout shorts. He didn't think she had a stitch of makeup on, and her blue eyes were as bright as the Mediterranean Sea.

He blinked as his jaw slackened and cleared his throat as he desperately tried not to look her up and down.

"What is this about selling the winery?" the lady asked.

"My mom has a buyer. That's why I came home. To help her with the negotiations."

The woman shook her head vigorously. "That is not what she told me." She stuck out her hand. "May I please speak with her?"

His mother was yelling in his ear that there had been a misunderstanding and about poor communication and a bunch of other things he really didn't understand. "Mom. Please be quiet for one second." He held up his hand. "I'm sorry. What's your name?"

The woman pursed her lips and glared. "If you must know, it's Eliza Jane Blue."

"Mother. What exactly did you do, and why am I here? Because I get the distinct feeling that both Eliza Jane and I are stuck in the middle of one of the manipulations you honestly believe are in everyone's best interests."

The phone went dead.

"Shit." He tossed his cell onto the sofa and plopped himself on the recliner. "Is it too early to start drinking?" He rubbed his temples. "When did my mom hire you?"

"I'm not sure I should discuss my employment contract with you." She scooted across the room and took down a couple of mugs, waving one in his direction.

"This might help you spill the details." He nodded at her unasked question. "My mom asked me to come home because she decided she couldn't run this place any longer and said she found a buyer and wanted my help with the details."

"I think that calls for a shot of Baileys." She pulled down a bottle from one of the cabinets and added it to the coffee. "I started working last week. My contract is for a year. If things work out, I get to stay on and start my own label under The River Winery. If none of you kids want this place, I have an option to buy—or at the very least stay on, since it's apparent that you don't want it." She waved her hand. "I don't mean to be rude, but since we're in this very awkward position, I might as well be honest at this point."

"Jesus. My mother is fucking brilliant."

"What the hell is that supposed to mean?"

Eliza Jane handed him the large mug and sat on the sofa.

He couldn't help but admire her pure beauty. She was stunning. Breathtaking. He wouldn't dare describe her as *model-like*. That would be too insulting. She was natural, and he suspected that she had the ability to fit in wherever she went.

"I'm not sure what my mom's end game is, but she's either trying to force my hand, bringing me home to run The River Winery, or she has something even weirder in mind. It's the latter that absolutely terrifies me." Mostly because if they weren't in Candlewood Falls, and his mother wasn't involved, he'd be inclined to ask Eliza Jane out on a date.

But that would never happen. It couldn't because his mother meddled way too much in his personal life. She meant well, but it never *ended* well.

"What do you mean?"

"Did she run an ad for a new winemaker? Did you apply for this job?"

"No. She pursued me."

"I can't believe my father let her do this." Malbec took a large gulp of his coffee, enjoying the burn and the alcohol. He laughed. "What the hell am I thinking? My dad couldn't have stopped her if he tried."

"I'm really lost."

"And I'm really sorry that you got stuck in the middle of this twisted game." He leaned forward. "Are you interested in purchasing my family's winery?"

"Maybe someday. But I'm not in a position to do it now."

"That's too bad. Because I need to talk my mother into selling it. She can't handle it anymore and—"

"That's why she hired me."

"No," Malbec said. "She's playing matchmaker. She knows the kind of woman I'm attracted to, and she went out and found one that fits both the bill in the looks department and probably in the brains and everything else department, too."

Eliza Jane bolted to her feet. "I seriously doubt that. And you're one egotistical man."

"Again. No. I just know my mother. She likely hoped that by bringing me home under the pretense that she'd found a buyer, I'd meet you, get all lovestruck, and maybe a little jealous over what you're doing here at what is my family's winery, and then I'd move back. That's all she's ever wanted."

"That's the craziest thing I've ever heard."

"That's my mom. I love her to pieces, but she does some really insane things, all in the name of what she thinks is best for her family. Sadly, it's driven most of us away."

"Well, I'm not leaving," Eliza Jane said, puffing out her chest.

"Okay. But I'm going to find a buyer for this place. My mom can't do it anymore, and I know my dad is done with it. It might have been in the family for generations, but all good things must come to an end, and The River Winery has run its course." He set the mug on the coffee table. "I'm sorry I barged in on you. Thanks for the coffee. I'm sure I'll see you around while I'm in town." He nodded. "Have a wonderful day." Now, it was time to go hunt down his mother. He had a few choice words for her, and for the first time in his life, he wouldn't let her tug his ear—or chew him out or have the last word.

Weezer

Weezer tapped the red button on her cell phone screen and set it on the nightstand. "I really fucked up this time." She heard Carter's feet hit the floor as he slipped from the bed. She glanced over her shoulder. "Aren't you going to tell me you told me so? Or give me some big lecture on meddling?"

"Nope, because I went along with it when I knew it would blow up in your face." Carter hiked up his jeans and planted his hands on his hips. "But now I am going to fix this fucking mistake. Hopefully, we won't lose our son for good this time." He yanked open one of the dresser drawers and pulled out a T-shirt. Carter didn't drop the F-bomb.

Ever.

As a matter of fact, the last time Weezer had heard him use the cuss word had been the day she'd told him that she wanted a divorce. That she thought they'd be better off living separate lives. He'd always been so damn understanding, and that bugged the shit out of her, though she had no idea why. Maybe it was because her father had been such a bastard to her mother, or perhaps it was because her dad had told her a million times that she didn't deserve a man like Carter.

Hell if she knew why she'd spent half her life pushing the only man that ever truly loved her away, and then her own flesh and blood. But it was high time she stopped the madness.

Only she kept going back to the only behavior she'd ever known. It had saved The River Winery from ruin when her father and grandfather owned it. And she'd kept up the façade. She thought she had to; because if anyone knew the truth about the winery, she could lose everything.

And she couldn't let that happen.

"Carter," she said softly. "I know I screwed up, but I thought I'd be able to fix it before it blew up in my face. I didn't think Malbec would come home a day early and show up at the cottage unannounced."

"He's a good man, and I bet he wanted to surprise you. He's got a kind heart that way. And now, he's pissed." Carter ran a hand through his salt-and-pepper hair. "And, frankly, I don't blame him. We shouldn't have lied to him."

"I know," Weezer said as she found her robe and cinched the tie tight around her waist. "I thought if—"

"I know what you thought, and I told you it wouldn't work. But as always, you had to do things your way." Carter tucked in his shirt and raked a hand through his hair. "I love you. I always have, and I always will. But you've gone too far this time, and you're going to have to let me take care of this. I'm going to call him and invite him for breakfast. I suggest you head on back to your place and smooth things over with Eliza Jane." He lowered his chin and narrowed his stare. "Because if you don't, our divorce will actually be a real one." He turned on his heels and disappeared out the door.

For the first time in her adult life, she didn't know what to do. Her grandfather would have told her to ignore Carter's words and form her own plan—or to revise her original one. Her father would have agreed. The winery had to stay within the family. She could never sell it.

And the Blue family could never, ever be involved. What her great-grandfather had done was in the past. It couldn't be undone. So the secret might as well stay buried. For years, she'd believed that and did whatever she had to in order to carry on what she felt was the River family tradition.

Only it was a lie, plain and simple.

But it was time to right the wrong her family had done generations ago.

4

MALBEC

Malbec would have preferred to have found his mother, but perhaps it was best if he had a few moments to cool his jets and have a nice breakfast with his dad. His father had a way of helping him understand his mom, or at the very least, the situation. He sat at the back patio table and stared into his coffee.

He couldn't get Eliza Jane out of his mind. Her beauty was undeniable, but it wasn't just that. There was something else about her that he found incredibly attractive, and he wanted to get to know her better. She seemed like the kind of woman he'd like.

But his mother had ruined that for him.

Besides, he planned to change his flight and leave as soon as he visited with all his siblings. He wouldn't just run off without seeing them—that would be rude. And, besides, he wanted to catch up with all of them.

He'd missed them. Being part of a large family was something Malbec both loved and hated. Growing up, it had truly been both a blessing and a curse. He never had any privacy—always having to share a room with Merlot, no matter what house they chose to stay at. But the second he went off to college, he'd missed his siblings. His roommate wasn't his family, and he preferred the kitchen table and his mother's cooking to cafeteria food.

"Here you go." His father set a plate of his famous French toast and bacon on the table.

"Thanks, Dad." He glanced up. "Did you know what Mom was up to?"

His father nodded and then lowered his gaze as if he were ashamed. "She promised me that she was going to tell you the truth as soon as you landed, but you came home early and met Eliza Jane before she had the chance."

Malbec shook his head. "That was quite the embarrassing introduction for both Eliza Jane and me."

"I can only imagine," his father said.

"Do you believe that Mom was going to come clean with her ruse?"

His father lifted his chin. "I do. But I'm also angry with myself for letting her do this. And it wasn't just about wanting you to run the winery. That, I'm totally on board with and have no issue with your mom playing her little games. I want you back in Candlewood Falls. This is your home. You belong here, and you belong at The River Winery."

A smile tugged at Malbec's lips. He shook his head. "What makes Eliza Jane so special that Mom thinks I'd give up my career in Napa Valley and move home to run the winery with her? Because that's what she's expecting now, isn't it?"

His father shrugged. "You're both talented viticulturists and vintners. You know our wines, and Eliza Jane has done wonders for failing wineries across the southwest. She has quite the reputation."

"I did a quick Google search on Eliza Jane this morning. Her record is both interesting and impressive." Malbec wasn't sure *interesting* was the right word, but it was the first one that came to mind. As did *sexy* and *sweet* and *smart* and a slew of other adjectives that confused him. But he doubted his father wanted to hear those. Nor did he want to contemplate them because that meant he'd have to examine the feelings stirring in his brain, gut, and heart for a woman he barely knew. That was something he had no intention of doing when he planned to get on a plane and go back to California as soon as he got his mother to listen to reason. "She's never stayed anywhere longer than eighteen months. That's barely long enough to understand anyone's process. That's so important if you really want to start your own line."

"That's not really true and you know it." His father

raised his mug and took a slow slip of his coffee while he arched his brow with that all knowing stare.

Malbec hated that at his age his father could still give him that look, and he'd be reduced to a small child in a matter of seconds.

"What's your real problem and let's not talk about the fact you think you want us to sell." His father set his mug down and cut into his French toast.

Sometimes Malbec resented his father's ability to always remain calm, no matter what. It was insanely annoying.

"But we do have to have that conversation because when we do find a buyer, and it will be a major company, Eliza Jane most likely won't be able to put her name on any label. She doesn't have the clout or the long-term experience. And have either you or mom considered what will happen when Eliza Jane decides she's done all she can here and moves on to the next vineyard? Because that's what she does and that only postponing the inevitable."

His father dropped his fork. "Do not insult me, son." He cleared his throat as he lifted his utensil and cleaned off the syrup. "And don't treat me or your mother as if we don't know what we're doing."

Shit. That was not what Malbec was trying to do. Well, not with his father anyway. "Dad. That's not what I meant. I'm just saying that Eliza Jane has a pattern of not staying anywhere for any length of time. That tells me she doesn't have the commitment to stick with creating a line of wines."

"You don't know her story," his father said with a deep tone. "So, until you get to know her, you don't get to make judgments."

Malbec had to admit that was fair to a point. He also would have to accept that he was looking for reasons not to find Eliza Jane fascinating. The more he distrusted her, the less he'd want to get to know her, only his father wasn't helping.

"You obviously know things I don't and you seem to think Eliza Jane and I are some kind of cosmic perfect match just like Mom."

His father laughed waving his hand. "I never said I believed Faith's vision."

"Excuse me? What about Faith?"

"Oh. You hadn't heard that?" His father shifted his seat. "Yeah. Well. I never said I believed it. I just agree with your mother that you and Eliza Jane would make for a great team. She's got your zest and excitement when she's in the vineyard. I can see it deep in her soul when she's working with the grapes and tasting the wine. She's a natural. She's you."

"You really think Mom found a match for me?" Malbec stared into his father's blue eyes. They were much lighter than the rest of the family's and often had a green tint. His mother used to tell all of the kids that a person could see into someone's soul through their eyes, and that's what attracted her to their father.

Malbec could see a deep passion in Eliza Jane. But he also saw a sense of loneliness.

Not the kind that made someone sad, but the kind that came from either being lost or from when a person ran from something. He knew this because, deep in his heart, he understood what that felt like.

And while it drove him nuts that his mother constantly tried to find him the perfect mate, in a far corner of his heart, the romantic in him kind of hoped his mom had that power.

"Your mother is scary intuitive when it comes to these things, and I've always trusted her when it comes to the winery." His father lifted his index finger. "Except when she all but ran you out of town. That said, yes, I like Eliza Jane, and she has some intriguing ideas that I believe will help bring The River Winery back to its glory. However, she's going to need help." His father ran his thumb and forefinger across his square chin. "To be honest, son, I think your mom has been trying to let these last few years of wine be a little less than perfect to see if you'd come home. But all it's done is make you want to sell, and that's not something I can let you continue to pursue. Not on my watch."

Malbec's jaw dropped open. That wasn't a scenario he'd ever considered. His mom was a lot of things, but to sabotage her family's long-standing reputation with their wines wasn't something he'd ever thought she'd do. No. He figured she was simply getting on in years, and the vineyard and winery were becoming too much for her to handle. And without a single River in sight to take it over, it was time to let it go. He let out a long breath. "Is she ready to tell me the big secret?"

"You'll have to ask her that." His father lowered his chin. "And don't keep pushing me on this because you know I'm not going to get in the middle."

"Fine. I'll drop it for now." Malbec rubbed his temple. His father always took his mom's side when it came to whatever this big, dark secret was, and it drove Malbec insane. "What else does Eliza Jane want? Because having her own label can't be her only end game." He decided it was best to move onto the next topic.

"Nothing has been signed," his father said. "The first year is all about seeing if we're a good fit. If she is, then we're looking at a percentage of the profits."

"Are you talking ownership?" Malbec's heart squeezed.

"I think this is a discussion we need to have when your mom is present."

"No. I want to know the details. And since I was once again manipulated to come home, I'd appreciate some answers."

"A small piece of the winery is part of the negotiation. But I believe Eliza Jane is more focused on her own label than ownership, if that makes you feel any better." His father poured a hefty dose of syrup over his French toast and dug in. "Eat. This is getting cold."

Malbec followed suit. He closed his eyes as his tastebuds exploded at the maple flavor mixed with powdered sugar, cinnamon, and of course, the sourdough bread his dad had soaked in egg. There was nothing like it. He blinked. "Eliza Jane said that Mom sought her out. Why?"

"For the record, we've had a lot of turnovers lately, and your mom wanted to find someone who might stay put. Not to mention, she knows she can't do this much longer."

"Mom actually admitted that?"

"Not in so many words, but you know that. And she won't sell. She promised your grandfather that she'd never let it go, and if your mother is anything, she's good to her word." His father lowered his chin. "And I'll reiterate. I'm in agreement with your mother. Selling isn't an option."

"Dad. I can't believe you're being as unreasonable as she is," Malbec said. "The winery is either going to bankrupt the two of you, or us kids will end up selling it when you die." He nearly choked on the last word. Even thinking about the day his parents left this Earth brought a tear to his eye. No matter the distance and the problems between him and his mom, his parents—and his siblings—were his everything.

"You're being dramatic," his father said. "We're not even close to financial ruin."

"You will be if something doesn't change."

His father smiled widely. A little too wide. He

leaned back and clasped his hands behind his head. "Something did change. Eliza Jane showed up."

"I still don't understand what makes Eliza Jane so special for both the winery and me that Mother had to pull this epic stunt."

His father shifted, rubbing his hands on his jeans. Malbec hated it when his father did that. "I don't have a clue either."

"Bullshit." Malbec's father knew everything his mother did and why. They had no secrets. Not a single one. If there were bodies, his dad knew where they were buried. "Be straight with me. Something about Eliza Jane that has Mom believing the new girl in town's tarot card readings. Faith and her nana might actually be the real deal, but come on, Dad. What the hell is really going on here? Mom doesn't do things based on what a card or a vision says."

"All I know about Faith and her nana ran into your mother in town right after she had a Zoom meeting with Eliza Jane. Faith saw you and Eliza Jane in a vision." His father shrugged. "I don't know anything else, so you'll need to ask your mother that question."

Malbec planned on doing just that, but he also knew his mother, and she had a way of avoiding the truth—though she'd only downright lied to him a handful of times.

Getting him to come home this week had been one of them.

The rest of her little fibs had been more twists of

the truth so she could get her way. Otherwise, she just didn't tell him anything.

What had been worse was her unwillingness to bend, which was what had pushed her family away—that and her damn secret. Something that tore at Malbec's heartstrings.

Deep down, his mother was a kind and loving woman, and he wanted the mother he remembered. The mom that had tucked him in at night when he was a small boy.

Not the Weezer the town stared at and gossiped about.

Malbec swallowed the lump in his throat. He'd met Eliza Jane once and for all of an hour, but something about her had him unable to push her from his mind. The desire to see her again made him crazy because it didn't make sense. There was no reason to get to know her, and yet, he knew the first chance he got, he was going to do just that. "I asked you to be honest. You said Eliza Jane and I would make for a good working relationship. Do you think we're a match personally?"

His father laughed. "She's the only young lady I've met that I think could handle you, so yeah. I do. But what I think doesn't matter." He tapped his chest. "If it's meant to be, then it will happen. Your mom and I are proof of that."

"I've never understood your relationship with Mom."

"It's not for you to understand, except to know that

we love each other and you kids." His father lifted a piece of bacon and shoved it into his mouth. "Your mom is trying to change."

Malbec laughed. "This doesn't feel like change."

"You're right. It doesn't. It's more like one giant leap backward. But she knows it, and that's a step in the right direction." His father wiped his fingers on his napkin and took a sip of his coffee. "Do me a favor and don't make any decisions about leaving just yet. I don't like what your mom did, and I told her as much. But as your grandpa used to say, what's done is done. No use sitting in shit. Might as well change the smell."

Malbec laughed. "Where the hell did he come up with those sayings? Half the time, they didn't even make sense."

His father raised his mug. "I have no damn clue. My father-in-law scared the crap out of me half the time. He was worse than Weezer. He was your mother on crack. But the same thing can be said about your mom that can be said about your grandfather. She's totally misunderstood, and while she might do some crazy-ass stuff, her heart is always in the right place."

Malbec couldn't argue that point.

"She has to come clean about the secret," Malbec said.

"Perhaps you need to change your approach in order to get the answers you seek."

"Does it have anything to do with this EJ man Grandpa rambled on about on his death bed?"

"Have you asked your mom about EJ?"

Malbec nodded. "She said she had no idea who he was and that maybe it was someone from Grandpa's childhood. Or just the dementia speaking."

"Ask her again, but do it in a different way," his father said. "Your mother is tired of all this, but it's hard for her. She made promises, and she's lived her life by your grandfather's rules. That hasn't been easy. That said, she never wanted any of you kids to have that same pressure."

"Jesus, Dad. You could put us all out of our misery by telling me what you know."

His father shook his head. "I can't do that. It's not my place. I'm sorry that it hurts you and that you don't understand, but I can't—I *won't*—do that to your grandfather's memory or to my wife." He held up his hand. "However, I do agree that she should tell you, so I will plead your case."

That was better than nothing. "I appreciate that."

"It's been eating your mother alive."

"Is it that bad?"

"Son, it's not good, and it will need to be handled with a delicate hand." His father leaned forward. "And it's a family matter." His dad arched both brows. "Family only."

Malbec swallowed. If his father wanted something to stay in the closet, it had to be worse than bad.

Eliza Jane

Eliza Jane swirled the red wine and brought it to her nose. She tried not to purse her lips at the acidic scent. It would be too harsh going down, and the palate of a wine connoisseur would absolutely reject this blend. It wasn't the worst flavor in the world, and at less than twenty dollars a bottle, it would probably do just fine. But this sold for over sixty. She had no idea how The River Winery stayed in business.

It didn't matter that this was their most inexpensive line.

It wasn't a good wine.

She couldn't even chalk it up to being a bad year. It simply hadn't been processed properly, and that didn't make much sense to Eliza Jane.

The door to the winemaking room squeaked open, and she glanced over her shoulder.

Weezer.

Oh, this conversation should be fun.

"Good morning," Eliza Jane said. "I was hoping you'd show up soon."

"I owe you an explanation." Weezer strolled in wearing a pair of jeans, a flannel shirt, her combat boots, and of course, perfectly styled hair and makeup. She truly was a beautiful woman, but she was a walking contradiction. She had a tough-as-nails exterior with an intimidating personality. However, it took a lot to frighten Eliza Jane.

Now, Malbec? He utterly terrified her, but for very different reasons.

"I should say so." Eliza Jane set the wine glass down, folded her arms across her chest, and leaned against the counter. She'd been in Candlewood Falls for a week and had barely had a chance to settle in. She'd known she'd meet the prodigal son at some point; she'd just hoped it would be long after she'd had the chance to feel secure in her position at the winery. "Besides being scared that someone had broken into the cottage, I'm concerned about my future and what you promised me. So, I need you to be straight with me because your son is adamant that he's selling The River Winery."

"He has no authority to do so," Weezer said. "Carter and I own it, so unless Malbec can somehow find me incompetent and get my husband to agree to sell, it's impossible." She pulled up a stool, took the glass, and brought it to her nose. "Jesus. What was I thinking? This isn't good."

"It's not the worst."

"But it's not up to my standards," Weezer said, letting out a long breath. "I owe you an apology."

"I've heard through the grapevine that Weezer River never apologizes."

"You heard wrong." Weezer smiled. "I almost never say I'm sorry. But I do when I do something wrong.

However, you're going to have to keep this to yourself. We can't go having the world believing I've gone soft." She waggled her finger. "Otherwise, I might have to take it back."

"Okay." This had to be the worst apology ever, but the fact that she was getting one at all, especially considering everyone had told her that Weezer would screw her over, said something about how the world might not know the real Weezer. "I'll keep it to myself if your explanation is to my satisfaction. And if my contract is still intact."

"Fair enough," Weezer said. "First, I'll tear up that contract and give you a permanent job right now. I know you're good. You don't have to prove yourself to me. And you can make your own wine with your name on it. But remember, it can't be one that we already make. Obviously, because of my kids. Or one that my grandfather used make because I'd like you to bring those back. It was a mistake to ever retire those blends. I only did so because I couldn't handle the production. But with you here, we can grow that process together with Malbec."

Eliza Jane opened her mouth because no way was Malbec getting in her way, but Weezer cut her off.

"I did use you, and I did lie to my son. I told him that I found a buyer, just to get him to take time off work and come home. I thought he'd become jealous of your skill and worry that he could lose all of this and want to be a part of it again." She lifted both her hands, palms to the ceiling. "And I hoped that some sparks would fly, and he'd stay home for good this time."

"That's quite a tall order." Eliza Jane's pulse kicked into high gear. She didn't know whether to laugh or hightail it back to the west coast. This had to be the most absurd scheme she'd ever heard.

However, she had to admit; she was insanely flattered that Weezer held her in such high regard.

On all accounts.

"I should quit," she stated boldly. "I don't like games."

"I wouldn't blame you if you did. But I'd like you to stay. I know it's going to take a couple of years to turn this place around, but we can do it." Weezer lifted her finger. "However, I have one condition."

Eliza Jane might have a few of her own. "What's that?" She swallowed. She'd been warned about how ruthless Weezer could be.

"If you ever decide you want to leave The River Winery, then the Eliza Jane Blue label, or whatever you decide to call it, stays with this winery. You can't take it with you." Weezer arched a brow. "You'd be using my grapes. And the process would be developed here. It's only fair."

Essentially, Eliza Jane would agree to stay in Candlewood Falls forever.

Or give up her name if something happened.

And she'd promised her father on his death bed that when she *did* find the right winery to make the perfect blend, her name would be displayed proudly on the bottle. It had been so important to her father and she would honor him that way.

That request had seemed to come out of the blue, but there were so many things about her family's history that she didn't understand. Besides, her great-grandfather had the talent and the passion.

He just didn't have the disposition.

"I can accept that part of the deal," Eliza Jane said. "What percentage of the label are we talking about?"

"Equal partners," Weezer said. "Only I won't have a single say in how you make your wine. It's just I'll be funding it."

"I think that's fair," Eliza Jane said. "However, I need to have more skin in the game." Her heart beat so fast, she thought it might jump right out of her chest. She hadn't expected to be negotiating this part of the deal for at least a year, but if they were going with a more permanent situation, then there was no way she was moving forward without knowing Weezer's intention.

And getting it in writing.

"What kind of skin are we talking?"

"Two and a half percent in a year. Five percent in five years. Ten percent in seven years."

"That's a lot of skin in my winery."

"I will be the one doing most of the work," Eliza Jane said. "And it needs to be done in a way that if anyone sells, my portion can't be sold with it. So, I will either have to be bought out or be taken along for the ride."

"I'll have to discuss that with Carter and all my children since this affects them, too, before I agree and put it in writing, but I think we can come to terms."

"You do that, and we've got ourselves a deal."

And that sealed her fate.

Now, all she had to do was make sure Malbec stayed the hell out of her way. That might be easier said than done.

"Good. I'm glad we understand each other."

"One more thing." Eliza Jane rubbed her hand over her thigh. Every night before she went to bed, she glanced at the image of her great-grandfather. And every night, she got the feeling that whoever had snapped the picture had been right at the river's edge where Weezer had said the family had planted the very first grapevines.

"I wouldn't get too greedy, young lady. I'm not a very generous woman, and this is going to be difficult to sell to my family."

"This isn't about asking for anything more," Eliza Jane said. "I'm curious about the year the vineyard was established, and when the first grapevines were planted."

"Oh, boy. I can't even remember the year my kids were born." She rubbed the back of her neck. "My grandfather started out as an illegal bootlegger, so it's sort of hard to pinpoint a date. It's why the grapes are so far back by the river."

"Bootleg wine?" Eliza Jane asked. "I get that during the prohibition. But that wouldn't have been your grandfather's time, would it?"

"No. But he made whiskey and wine and sold it, avoiding the taxes, therefore making it illegal. I don't know exactly what year he went legit. I'd have to look it up."

"So, the first few years, The River Winery was illegally run, and your family avoided paying money to the government. That's very interesting. I'm surprised that's not a story the world talks about."

"That's because it's not the narrative we want the world to know. And you're not going to repeat it, now, are you?" Weezer hopped off the stool and didn't give Eliza Jane a chance to answer. "Why don't we take the barrels that we have left of that particular blend and use them for cheese pairings at some of the upcoming festivals and to sell as cooking wines. That should take care of some of our issues, and you can get to work making great wines." Weezer turned and glanced over her shoulder. "And while Malbec is here, take advantage of his abilities. I'm sure you're just as good as he is, but two great minds could do a lot together—even if only for one week."

She got the feeling that Malbec was a lot like his mother and not very hands-off. "Are you going to give him any control, even from a distance?"

"He's smart, and I value his opinion." She waggled her finger. "You'd be a fool not to tap into that brain of his no matter where in the world that boy of mine is. Now, if anyone comes looking for me, I'm off to chase that damn Alpacino back through the fence. Stupid alpaca manages to find its way onto the vineyard all the time." Weezer practically skipped out of the room.

Eliza Jane shook her head. She suspected that the woman pretty much got whatever she wanted.

And then some.

However, she did want to find out more about the history of the vineyard and winery. She didn't care about what Weezer's grandfather did in the past.

She'd just turned her attention back to the task at hand when the door squeaked again. "What did you for —? Oh. Hi, Malbec." She blinked a few times, trying to catch her breath. It annoyed her that a man had this kind of effect on her mind and body.

But it was worse that it was Malbec.

Especially since she'd only known him for a day.

While he wasn't the enemy, at least according to Weezer, he hadn't entered the room with a beaming smile.

As a matter of fact, he didn't look happy at all. His lips were drawn into a tight line, and his brow was furrowed. "Hey, Eliza Jane. Have you seen my mom?"

"She just left like ten minutes ago. Said something about an alpaca named Alpacino?"

Malbec's blue eyes went from dull pools of darkness

to a sparkling drink of water in seconds. He ran a hand through his thick, dark hair. "I swear she's in love with that darn animal. I can't tell you how many times I've found her down there talking to it. My dad once told us that if she ever left him for real, it would be for an alpaca."

"They're funny-looking creatures."

"You can say that again. But you have to admit, they are kind of cute in their own odd way."

"If you say so." In order to keep her mind on anything other than the man standing way too close, causing a warm blanket of heat to spread across her skin, she continued to bottle the tasting and cooking wines. One of the things that had enticed her to come work at The River Winery was their unique way of doing business. While they sold their wines to liquor stores and restaurants across the country, they also did a lot of local festivals and tastings, and they weren't afraid to think outside of the box, creating an entire line of specialty wines just for cooking and pairings they used at special local events only. It really gave them a hometown feel.

Just like their tagline.

Small town. Big taste.

"Here. Why don't you let me help you?" Malbec stood next to her and began corking and labeling. While they used a big plant to do the bulk of their bottling, these specialty items were done by hand. It was a nice and special touch to be able to put personal labels on each bottle.

"You don't have to."

"I don't mind. Besides, I wanted to say I'm sorry for barging in on you this morning," he said as he pulled down the level.

"It was an honest mistake."

He nodded. "That is true. But I was rude and said some things that I shouldn't have."

"Yes. You were. But so was I. You caught me off guard with the things you were saying. However, I've since spoken to your mother, and we're all good." She glanced in his direction. "I'm not leaving. And your mother isn't selling." She swallowed the lump in her throat. Normally, she wasn't afraid to speak her mind, but Malbec managed to twist her stomach into knots.

"Just so you know, I'm going to do everything in my power to talk her into it, and I'm going to discuss it with people I know in the business. There are some large wineries that would love to buy this place. What-ever agreement you have with Mom, I will do my best to ask them to honor it. But you know how these large companies are."

One of the bottles slipped from Eliza Jane's fingers.

He bent over and managed to grab it before it smashed into a million pieces on the wood floor.

But not before red wine spilled all over her jeans.

"Shit," she mumbled as she snagged a cloth from the counter and patted herself down.

Unfortunately, Malbec had done the same thing.

Awkwardly, she batted his hand away.

"Let me help," he said softly as he took a cloth and swiped at her thighs.

"I've got it." She reached for the towel. A soft, lingering sensation coated her skin. It felt like a warm, fuzzy blanket on a cool fall day as she snuggled in front of a fireplace, eagerly awaiting the very first snowflake to fall from the sky. It was always the anticipation of what might happen, and part of her wished she hadn't pushed him away and let him clean up the wine that soaked into the fabric now sticking to her legs.

"Why would start a conversation with major liquor corporations?" She took a step back and glared. She needed to focus on the problem and now how badly she wanted to feel his lips on hers, because that would only make this situation worse.

"Because they acquire small wineries like this all the time," he said. "The vineyard I work at used to be a small, family-owned operation. But ten years ago, Venture Liquors bought it out. At the same time, they snatched up the surrounding land and expanded the vineyard. It's really given us the opportunity to become a household name. Not to mention, the original owners are sitting pretty financially."

"Not everything comes down to money, and you run the risk of ruining your family's special blends. You know they will come in and change the process, and the flavor of your wines will change as a result. They will never be the same."

"My mother's already screwed that up." He waved the bottle in her face. "Can't you smell that? It's nearly ruined."

She inhaled sharply and closed her eyes for a long moment. She couldn't deny what was literally right under her nose. "Yes," she whispered. "But—"

"No buts. My mother has let this place go, and it will take years to rebuild the wines and our reputation if we remain a small family-run operation."

She narrowed her stare and poked him in the chest. "And whose fault is that?"

"Are you saying it's mine?"

"You're the one who went off to Napa Valley for some corporate winery job and left your mother to fend for herself, aren't you?" She couldn't believe the words that flew from her lips. She didn't know this man or his history with his family. She only knew what others said. And she, of all people, should know that it could be a bunch of misunderstandings and half-truths, considering what the world had thought about her great-grandfather.

"Are you kidding me? I make one of the finest wines in the country."

"Just because it costs a pretty penny doesn't mean it's all that great. And does it have your name on it? No. Did you create it? No. You follow a recipe that has been in place for how many years now?"

"I tweak it from year to year. Just like we do here."

"Your mother created seven fresh blends all on her own. And before that, your grandparents created six blends. And let's not forget the whiskey that came out of this winery during the prohibition. The River Winery is a leader. All you do is follow the herd." She brushed her hair from her face. "I'd rather be a pioneer than just another cog in the machine." She tossed the rag onto the counter and stormed out of the room, wishing she knew where the hell this alpaca named Alpacino was.

He sounded like he might be a good listener.

5

MALBEC

"A cog in the machine?" Malbec whispered as he followed her outside and around the building. There was no way that Eliza Jane had just said that to him, had she? Well, he had something to say about that. "Eliza Jane, wait." He jogged down the path and skidded to a stop, bringing his hand to his forehead as the sun nearly blinded him.

A flash of dark hair waved in the distance as Eliza Jane took off running toward where the riverbend and the water met the alpaca farm.

Looked as if she might actually want to have a chat with Alpacino.

Wonderful.

What the hell did that animal have that the River men didn't?

"Eliza Jane," he called as she wove through the rows

of vines. "You don't get to say those things and just take off."

She turned. "Oh, yes, I do." She planted her hands on her hips. "And unless you want to know what I really think of you and your plans, I suggest you leave me alone."

He wasn't sure if he wanted to take her in his arms and kiss her or give her a piece of his mind.

Both were equally appealing for different reasons.

He sucked in a slow breath and counted to ten. Something his father told him to do when he wanted to be like his mom and go off at the mouth.

Only this time, it had to do with controlling his desire to kiss the hell out of this woman, and that kind of made no sense. He shouldn't be turned on by being insulted.

He closed the gap so he stood only two feet away. "You can believe whatever you want about me and how my leaving for Napa affected my family and this winery. But you don't know me or my mom or the history, so you're honestly talking out of your ass." He reached out and covered her mouth with his hand. "There's no point in saying another word on that subject. We'll have to agree to disagree."

She shoved his hand away. "Then why are we standing here, obviously having an argument?" She arched a brow.

"Because if you want to make your own label, you have to be a cog. And if you can't accept that, you'll never survive in this business." He had to bite back a smile as the look on her face went from tense and angry to tight and confused.

Eliza Jane was the sexiest woman he'd ever met, and she didn't even have to try. She had this natural ease about her that screamed confidence.

However, she had a lot to learn about longevity in winemaking.

She narrowed her eyes, and the crinkles etched in her forehead grew longer and wider. "What the hell are you babbling about? You don't know shit about being creative and trying to master a new blend. Nor do you care."

"Oh. And you know this about me?"

"Of course, I do." She brushed the hair that had blown in front of her face away. "I've worked for three very large, corporate vineyards, and I've met a few winemakers just like you."

"What the hell does that mean?"

"It's simple," she said. "You're comfortable making quality. But you're not willing to take a risk."

"That's bullshit." Who the hell was this woman to give him this psychobabble crap? "And while that might be true for all those other winemakers, it's not for me." He turned on his heels and took three steps before stopping and marching right back to her until his nose was only inches from hers. "Growing up as Weezer's son in Candlewood Falls was hard enough. Going out into the wine business was even harder. Do you know that some wineries wouldn't even give me an interview because of whose kid I was?"

"Why wouldn't they want to have a conversation?"

"Because they thought my mom sent me to steal their secrets, or that I wasn't serious about being in their employ for any length of time. When I finally landed a job, I was underpaid and given all the shit work. I literally started in a position we'd get summer help for."

"I'm sorry you struggled," she said. "But you've paid your dues and are in that nice, cushy job without any risk now. I just don't understand why you don't want to create your own blend and put your name on it. Especially when you have the resources to do it."

"Are you serious right now?" He sucked in a deep breath and let it out slowly. He needed to rein in his anger and frustration. Getting in a fight with a woman that his parents both believed could help put their winery back on top, who was also his so-called perfect match, wasn't a good idea. He had to agree with his father about his mom's wicked intuition about certain things like people's love lives, but if she was listening to Faith's nana, well, that was a different story.

"Yes." Eliza Jane squared her shoulders. "Not that I want you here—"

"Gee. Thanks."

"I'm not going to even go there with you, and you know why." She planted her hands on her hips. "You have the world at your fingertips right here, and yet you chose to turn your back on all of it. And I don't understand why."

"Because my parents screwed me," he said, wishing he could take the words back the second they flew from his lips.

"What?"

He glanced at the sky. A big, white, puffy cloud danced across the sun's bright rays. He'd always loved the way the sun shone on the grapevines. It reminded him of a pot of gold at the end of a rainbow.

"From where I'm standing, your parents have given you everything," she said.

"Except the ability to put my name on a bottle of wine." He lowered his chin. "Not that I need that, because I don't. But you keep bringing it up. And for a long time, it was an issue for me. I mean, my name is Malbec. That is a bottle of wine. And my last name is on seven different blends." He pressed his finger to her plump lips when she tried to speak. "I never felt the need to create my own because the second I went out into the world, the industry looked at me as if I were some spoiled kid who'd just go running back to Mommy."

"Is that the real reason you haven't come back?"

"Anyone ever tell you that sometimes talking with you can cause whiplash?"

She let out a little chuckle. "I've been accused of that."

"Look. I know you think that I'm sticking my nose up at what I was born into—"

She poked his forearm. "You don't know me or what I'm thinking."

"Then tell me that's not true."

She blinked. Slowly. "Fine. That's exactly what I believe."

"And that's what a lot of people have thought about me over the years. But it's not true. Sure, when I first left, I was rebelling against my mom and even my grandfather for things you have no clue about—and I'm not going to tell you. It's family business. However, as I honed my skills, I realized something that my mom had been trying to beat into my head for years. And that's: You can't rush a good wine. It's ready whenever it tells you it is, and no matter where I work, or whose wine I make, my role is to make sure the wine has the proper tools to mature." He pounded his chest. "As arrogant as this sounds, without me, that wine has no chance. That's why I've been offered three jobs in the last eighteen months, and why my company gets nervous every time I come home."

"You're pretty full of yourself."

"I'm good at what I do."

"So am I," she said. "But I don't have the last name River." She held up her hand. "My turn to talk."

"All right."

"I get you might have had some hard knocks because of who your mother and grandfather and even great-grandfather are. Trust me. I understand that better than most. But the difference between you and me is that I use it as an excuse to take life by the horns and take chances with my talents." She waved her hand. "Your family grows some fine grapes. It's a shame you don't want to create a Reserve Malbec River blend that would put that fancy, expensive one your current employer makes to shame."

His heart raced, and his palms grew sweaty. It wasn't that he was worried he couldn't do it. He knew damn well that he could.

It all came back to that stupid secret. But he was as stubborn as his mother, and he wasn't about to cave.

"That's your opinion."

A slight breeze kicked up and brushed a few strands of hair in front of her face.

He reached out and gently tucked them behind her ear.

"Hey, Malbec? Is that you?" a male voice rang out.

He glanced over his shoulder. "Caleb?" It had been years since the man had been in town for anything more than a hot minute. "What the hell are you doing here?"

"Trying to buy a bottle or two of wine."

"I'll go take care of him." Eliza Jane took a step forward.

He curled his fingers around her forearm. "He's an old friend. I've got this."

"You don't work here." She pursed her lips.

"Whenever I'm home, I help out. And for as long as my parents own this place, that's not going to change. So, for the next week, I suggest you get used to seeing my face around here." He leaned in and kissed her cheek. "I'm also not going to stop having conversations with my family about selling, and I know I have my siblings on my side. It doesn't mean you won't be able to—"

"Your friend is waiting." She wiggled free. "I appreciate your help with him, but after that, make yourself scarce. Since I'll be slowly taking over some of the operational and management roles, I think it would be better if you didn't hang around. It will only confuse the employees."

This was going downhill again, and he didn't want to make it worse. But every time he opened his mouth, he put his foot in it. However, he wouldn't become invisible. He had every intention of being at the winery, every chance he got. "I'll be right there, Caleb," Malbec said. "We're not done talking." He spun a hundred and eighty degrees and made a beeline for the main building. He didn't dare glance over his shoulder for fear she might be hot on his heels. "So sorry to keep you waiting."

"Who's the hottie?" Caleb stretched out his arm.

"My mom's new manager," Malbec admitted, staring at Caleb's bruised face. "What the hell happened to you?"

"I had a make-out session with the pavement."

"It doesn't look like it was very good for you." Malbec held open the door.

"It wasn't good for my motorcycle, either. Which is why I'm still in this godforsaken town. I'm waiting for parts. Otherwise, I'd be long gone by now."

"I have to admit, I'm shocked to see you." Malbec found a nice bottle of merlot from a few years back. "This is a good year, and a fine blend, unless you're having fish. Then I'd go for a white."

"Nope. This will work." Caleb held the bottle in his scratched-up hand. "What brings you back?"

"My mom and her games."

"Oh. That sounds like fun. How is *the* Weezer? I have to admit, some of my fondest childhood memories are from some of our camping trips and her crazy antics."

"She's always entertaining, that's for sure." Malbec rang up the wine and put it in a bag. "Where are you staying?"

"That, you might not believe." Caleb stuffed his wallet into his back pocket.

Malbec arched a brow. "Are you staying with Brooklyn?"

"And that's why you got better grades than I did in school." Caleb held up the bag. "Don't take this the wrong way, but I hope I don't see you anytime soon. Because once my bike is fixed, I'm getting the fuck out of this town."

"I'll be right behind you."

Caleb laughed. "Not if that gorgeous lady continues turning your head. Though I suspect she's way out of your league."

"Brooklyn's out of yours."

"Ain't that the truth?"

Malbec leaned against counter and watched his old buddy limp out of the store. Caleb had gotten a raw deal. Merlot had decided to become a parole officer in part because of what had happened to Caleb years ago. It pained Malbec that this town hadn't been able to see the truth, especially when his mom had done her best to make sure everyone knew that Caleb hadn't done what he was accused of.

But this town had a long memory, and a few nasty people that didn't let the past go.

He groaned. Somehow, he needed to get his parents on the same page. It had to start with his father. If he could get his dad to see the value in selling, then they could all gang up on his mom.

With Eliza Jane in the mix, that seemed impossible, but he still had to try.

No, he had to *succeed*, and that was something that Malbec was very good at.

Eliza Jane

Eliza Jane spent the next two hours pacing in the vineyard as she waited for Malbec to leave the building. She didn't want to deal with him, mostly because she knew she'd say something she'd regret.

Again.

She just couldn't help herself when it came to Malbec. He had her all tied up in knots between the sexual tension and the frustration over the fact that he had no idea what he'd left behind. She had no right to judge him.

But she did.

She continued fiddling with displays, but she couldn't focus. Therefore, her creativity was out the window. She had a list of things to do a mile long. However, not a single one was getting done. Not today. Ugh. Malbec was proving to be a problem in more ways than one.

The bell on the door caught her attention.

A woman wearing an oversized hat, extra-large, round sunglasses, and a London Fog raincoat stepped into the shop. She didn't bother taking off her shades, but she did adjust them slightly.

"May I help you?" Eliza Jane asked as she peered out the window. A slight drizzle tickled the window-panes while the sun tried to peek through a single dark cloud that loomed in the blue sky.

"Are you in here all alone?" the woman asked.

That was an odd question, but Eliza Jane had decided that everyone in Candlewood Falls had idiosyncrasies. It was just a small-town thing, and she'd have to get used to it. And as long as she didn't develop any quirks, she'd be just fine. "I'm the only one in the gift shop, but we have other people at the winery. What is it you're looking for?"

The woman glanced around as she slowly waltzed between the displays, gliding her fingers across the tabletops. "Just a couple of bottles of the merlot, and maybe some cheese and snacks that are a good pairing."

"I can certainly help you with that."

"Are any of the Rivers here?"

"I'm sorry, not right now," Eliza Jane said. "Are you friends with the family?"

"We have a history." The woman removed her glasses.

"Oh. We met last week at the coffee shot."

The woman nodded. "I don't mean to be rude, but I'm in a bit of a hurry. I have a family obligation."

"No worries. About how many people will this be for?"

"Twenty."

"And you only want two bottles?" Eliza Jane pulled down six. "I can give you twenty percent off on the total purchase." She turned and opened the fridge, pulling out a medium-sized tray of cheeses and various fruits before finding crackers and some nuts to go with it. "This should be more than enough."

"Thank you. I really appreciate it."

nothing like small-town coffee, especially in Candle-wood Falls. Every time he entered the building, it smelled as if he'd walked into his childhood. It was a combination of coffee mixed with cinnamon, sugar, apples, and a dash of maple. It made his tastebuds come alive. No other coffee shop in the world had ever made his entire body jolt with just a single whiff. "I'll have whatever the person in front of me just ordered. It sounded awesome. Oh. And how about two of those pumpkin muffins?" His stomach growled.

"Coming right up," the young girl behind the cash register said. "You can wait over there." Malbec put his credit card in the reader and waited for his receipt.

"Malbec River? Is that you?" a male voice asked.

Malbec spun on his heels and stared at a familiar face. "Sam Wilde. Look at you, all grown up." Sam was about eight years younger than Malbec. Actually, he'd graduated a year after Merlot. While Sam and Merlot traveled in much different circles—Merlot being a hockey player, and Sam being, well, a nerd—Sam was a nice enough kid. And they had known each other for their entire lives, considering that Sam's family owned the local apple orchard, and the two businesses did many local festivals together.

Sam stretched out his arm.

Malbec took his hand in a firm handshake.

"I didn't know you were back in town," Sam said. "Are you here long?"

"Just a few days." Malbec didn't see the need to

elaborate, especially since his order had just been called. "I have to run. Say hello to the family for me."

"Will do. Have a great day," Sam said.

Malbec took his coffee and muffins and headed outside, finding a table where the three youngest siblings were already situated with their coffees, breakfast pastries, and long faces.

The youngest of the group, Zinfandel, was only twenty-two. She'd just graduated college last year with a degree in marketing and sales. She joined the twins, Nebbiolo and Pinot Noir—or Noir—who were twenty-six, in sales for the family business. Specifically, selling the wine. However, the winery didn't employ them. They worked for a local large corporation that carried many of the local liquors.

"I can't believe what Mom did," Zinfandel said before plopping part of her chocolate croissant into her mouth. Of all the girls, she was the most outspoken. Of course, she was the youngest. In order to get a word in with this group, she practically had to scream. But she held her own, and she was wicked smart.

"Are you kidding. You're the one who called it," Noir said. "Not to mention, she's been trying to find ways to get this guy home for ten years. And I, for one, can't blame her."

"Me, neither," Nebbiolo added. "We need you. Like, bad. Sales suck, and they are only going to get worse. Our reputation is shit, and the wine isn't getting any better."

"It's not that bad." Zinfandel took a sip of her fruity, blended tea drink, topped with extra whipped cream. The girl had a major sweet tooth, and she'd never developed a taste for coffee. She said it made her want to vomit. Of course, she'd said that about wine the first time she tried it and now she was an expert. "And this chick that Mom hired is good. As in about as good as you."

"Mom would never say that." Malbec cleared his throat.

"It's true." Nebbiolo waved his chocolate chip muffin in the air. "And she's got a head for business with a creative flare. She's like a little angel sent from the grape gods."

"But she's not you, and if you'd get your fucking head out of your ass, rein in that inflated California ego of yours, and come home where you belong, maybe this winery would have half a chance." Noir tossed in his two cents.

Malbec stared out at the main drag of town. Napa Valley was beautiful. One of the prettiest places he'd ever been. Between the rolling hills, the breathtaking sunsets, and the picture-perfect greenery, he loved living there.

But it wasn't this.

"What if Taubet Liquors were willing to buy The River Winery, keeping our brand intact? The three of you would still have jobs, and the rest of us would have stock in the company, plus a large sum of money from the sale." He'd called a few different contacts and three large liquor companies yesterday. Only one so far had any real interest, but if he could get one on the hook, he'd get more, and that could mean a bidding war.

However, the fact that there was interest at all told Malbec that he was onto something, and that gave him pause. He didn't like questioning his plan, and he'd need to spend some time thinking about why selling was so important and also going over the books. Plus, he *did* have three more siblings to sit down and talk with.

Nebbiolo dropped his muffin to the ground.

Noir's jaw gaped.

And Zinfandel's fruity drink slipped through her fingers to land on her white skirt—which was unfortunate.

"Did they make Mom an offer?" Noir asked after snapping his mouth shut.

Zinfandel scrambled to clean up the mess that would surely leave a stain, which would piss her off, and that was never a good idea.

Malbec wasn't having much luck over the last twenty-four hours, delivering ideas without causing a big ruckus. Of course, his sister Chablis always accused him of stirring the pot.

"No. But they aren't the only ones who are interested. I've made a couple of phone calls, but so far, Taubet is the only one willing to take a meeting."

"Jesus Christ. What do Mom and Dad think of all

this?" Nebbiolo asked. "Do they even know? Or should we just call you a Weezer in the making?"

Malbec rubbed his temple. He hated admitting that his little brother had a damn good point.

His mom had been an only child and had taken after her dad, the eldest of five. He'd been an ornery man and everyone in town called him Grizzly.

However, that was in part due to the beard he refused to shave.

Everybody had called Grizzly's father Bad Billy.

It was no wonder that everyone in town expected that one of the River kids would turn out just like their mother. Malbec had just hoped it wouldn't be him, but it wasn't looking good. He wondered what kind of nickname he might be given. As long as it wasn't *sour grapes*, he could handle about anything.

"I'm just trying to do what's best for this—fuck. Yes. I hear myself. And I get that I sound like Mom. But it's true." He pointed over his shoulder. You could see parts of the winery at the edge of the town. "Look at it. The buildings are run-down, and I took a walk around the grapevines. They aren't anywhere near as good as they were in years past. It's going to take more than a talented viticulturist and vintner to turn this ship around." Okay. So he exaggerated a little bit. He needed to do so to prove a point.

"You're right." Zinfandel stood. "It's going to take you." She slammed her empty plastic cup on the table. "I might be the baby, and you might be sixteen years older than me, but it's time you stop running from whatever it was that had your panties in a wad when you were my age. It's time to grow the fuck up, Malbec, and do what this family needs you to do. And that's not selling." She stormed off toward the coffee shop for what Malbec assumed was another sugar rush.

Like she needed one.

"You tell him, baby sis," Noir said, giving a little fist pump in the air.

"Don't encourage her." Malbec rolled his neck. This was not how he thought the morning would go. He'd figured of all his siblings, it would be these three who were tired of dealing with the bullshit.

But he was wrong.

Maybe he'd have better luck with the firefighter, the parole officer, and the physician's assistant.

God help him.

His family was a hodgepodge of eclectic personalities. While he was the only one who'd taken off for the other side of the country, they had all run from their parents in one way or another.

He was just the one with enough balls to sort of admit it.

And now they were all begging him to come home and save something they refused to take part in.

Okay. Well, at least the three youngest had a hand in the business. But they all had one foot out the door, selling wines and liquors for a large distribution chain.

They could give up on The River Winery if they wanted to—they were just too afraid of Weezer.

"Why not?" Noir said. "Someone has to tell you like it really is."

"Agreed." Nebbiolo leaned back and folded his arms across his chest. "We've all thought it. We just never vocalized it to you before. And you know how important it was to Grandpa to keep this in the family." Nebbiolo waved his index finger at Malbec. "And don't go tossing the dark secret around. Our great-grandfather is long dead. Whatever he told Grandpa and Grandpa told Mom, can't hurt us."

"We don't know that," Malbec said. "We've all seen what that secret has done to Mom."

"You staying away has done worse," Noir said. "And, come on. We all know the story about the box of secrets the old doctor hid somewhere near the overflow building, so that's not the only one this land has to offer."

"It's the only one that has driven a wedge between us, and the only one that Mom holds over my head." He was damn tired of this argument, and he wasn't about to discuss a box that probably didn't exist and was only brought up to deflect the issue that had the potential to destroy the winery and his family for good. "The way I see it, we have two choices." Malbec sipped his coffee for the first time. Damn, it was getting cold, but it was still the best brew he'd ever tasted. "We can sell it to a big company and watch it grow and profit and be proud of what our family has done. Or, we can sit back and watch it bankrupt Mom and Dad. Because that's what's going to happen if we do nothing. And then we'll all have nothing to show for our family's hard work. Is that what you want?"

Noir harshly pushed back his chair and stood. "Or we can all band together and make this winery great with you at the helm. And did you ever think that you might be able to do that at somewhat of a distance?"

"And Eliza Jane?" Nebbiolo added as he joined his twin. The two might not be identical in looks, but they were the only two in the family identical in personality. "She's a lot like you, and she's the best thing that Mom has done in years. With your guidance, she could run this place, and you might still be able to keep your stupid job in Napa Valley."

The sound of angry footsteps coming up behind him made him clench. His baby sister was a force to be reckoned with.

"Besides lying to get you to take a week off work, Mom didn't really do anything that any of us didn't want her to do," Zinfandel said. "So, don't be an asshole and go running off. At least talk with Eliza Jane. Listen to her ideas and have an open mind. And for the love of all things holy, pause all talks with those big companies."

Malbec blew out a puff of air. He could slow down the talks. Hell, he only had one company that had shown any real interest. But speaking with Eliza Jane might prove more difficult. "Okay, but there is one problem."

His sister jutted out her hip and brought her straw to her lips as she tapped her shoe against the pavement.

"Eliza Jane hates me," he said.

Zinfandel licked her lips. "That's because in your thirty-eight years on this planet, you still have no clue about women."

Malbec stifled a laugh. "Oh, and you do?"

"I am one, aren't I?"

"Barely," he mused but winced the second the words tumbled from his mouth.

Of all the girls, Zinfandel had more of his mother's quick wit. Not to mention, she had no filter.

"Shall I start talking about all my sexual exploits, vibrators, and—?"

He held up his hand. "Good God, no. That might be worse than being in the same house with Mom and Dad."

"Ew. Gross," the twins and his sister said collectively.

Zinfandel waved her hand. "My point is, you've never had much game. Truth is, you're not much better with the ladies than Sam Wilde."

"Damn. That hurt." Malbec knew his sister was teasing. He hoped. "I've had no problem getting dates, thank you very much."

His sister lowered her chin. "And how often do you date? When was your last serious relationship?"

"That has nothing to do with my ability to woo a girl."

"Prove it," Zinfandel said.

"How?" He shouldn't have asked the question.

The twins glanced between each other and then back at him. "Is she thinking what we think she's thinking?"

"That's a damn tongue teaser," he mumbled. "I'm not going to flirt with Eliza Jane, so you can forget that. It's stupid and pointless and has nothing to do with the problem at hand."

"It has everything to do with this situation," Nebbiolo said. "Especially if you're interested in helping to keep the winery in our family."

"Are you willing to do that?" Noir asked. "Because all of us are willing to do our shares."

Malbec liked the idea of The River Winery making a comeback, but only if it could be on his terms, and if his family could guarantee that it wouldn't be something they would do for a few years, only to get bored and put them back at square one. However, first, he'd have to get his mother to agree to step back and give him some control—and more than just a little.

She'd have to turn over all final decisions to him.

And that included the worth of Eliza Jane and her role at The River Winery.

It was either that or he'd go back to Napa Valley in a heartbeat.

However, he didn't need to go over those specific details right now with his siblings. That was a conversation to have with the entire family, and only after he got his mother to agree to putting him in charge.

And only if that happened from a distance.

If she agreed to that, he'd put a stop to his talks with the big wine companies.

"I'll entertain the concept." Malbec pushed his chair back and stood, curling his fingers around his uneaten bag of muffins.

Perhaps Eliza Jane might enjoy one.

"What does that mean exactly?" Noir asked. "Because sometimes you can be more vague than Mom."

"I'll make my decision on whether or not to commit to keeping the winery by Friday."

"That's in five days." Zinfandel cocked her head. "Can't you think any faster than that?"

"I'll let you know if my brain decides to work at warp speed." He patted his baby sister on the shoulder. "You kids have a good day selling wine. I'll be talking with you soon." He stuffed his free hand into his pocket and strolled toward his vehicle.

Time to bring his game to a new level.

7

ELIZA JANE

Eliza Jane found an old wooden dock on the river that ran by the winery. She kicked off her sandals and stuck her toes in the chilly waters. She never imagined that New Jersey could be this beautiful. She expected either skyscrapers in a city with a view of Manhattan, or the ocean shores with houses on top of one another and hard surfer bodies in tiny bathing suits drinking and partying like it was the end of summer every day.

She leaned back and stared at the water running over the shiny rocks. This spot really reminded her of that old black-and-white picture of her great-grandfather. But she knew it couldn't be. Her heart was only searching for someplace to call home. Since she and her father had moved from one place to the next until she turned fifteen, she'd never really felt rooted anywhere. She wanted to make this place her home. She'd projected her desire to feel a connection to her past on her deep-seated need to be grounded.

She let her thoughts wander back to the situation currently torturing her soul. Her mind raced with a million questions, and she desperately needed to take a moment and try to sort out all the possibilities of what Malbec's return could actually mean for her future. Having one viticulturist and vintner at a winery and vineyard this size, with the volume that it often produced, wouldn't cut it in years to come. Right now, she had Weezer and, on occasion, Carter.

The twins also knew a fair amount and were willing to help, but there was only one Malbec River.

She wondered if he knew about the rumors. The wine business wasn't as big as one might think. At least, when it came to growing and making. And many in the business believed that Malbec had run scared. That he'd taken a job in Napa because he didn't have what it took to follow in his mother's footsteps.

Well, Eliza Jane didn't believe it. He'd left long before the wine quality started to decline. She just couldn't understand why he wouldn't want to make a wine with his name on it. She rolled the explanation that he'd given her yesterday around in her head, and it was a concept she couldn't fathom. Sure, she didn't understand the family dynamics, and yes, that could change everything, but Malbec lived two thousand miles away.

Apart from a family he obviously loved, cared for, and wanted to have a good relationship with.

That just didn't jive with the things he'd stated.

Someone cleared their throat.

She jerked. "Shit. You scared me." She brushed her hair from her face, hoping her cheeks didn't turn red as Malbec strolled down the wobbly dock.

"Sorry." He held up a bag from the local coffee shop. "I brought a peace offering.

Her stomach growled. Anything from that place made her mouth water. "I didn't realize we were at war."

"I didn't like how we ended our last conversation."

"It was pretty intense," she admitted. "And I have a feeling we're going to be at odds for as long as you're here." She took the tasty treat he offered as he sat down beside her, slipping off his shoes and rolling up his jeans as if he'd sat in this very spot a million times.

Of course, he likely had. He'd lived here for his entire childhood.

"That may be true." He laughed. "I will try to be on my best behavior from here on out."

"I'm sorry for the way I behaved yesterday, especially for accusing you of ruining your family business. I could have handled that situation differently."

"I won't disagree, but I also tend to come in hot." He took a large bite of his muffin.

She dropped her gaze to hers and fiddled with the wrapper, taking only small nibbles. She wasn't sure how to continue this conversation. He made her uncomfortable and not because of the business.

Because of how attracted she'd become not only to his body but also his intellect and his witty personality. There were more layers to Malbec than met the eye, and if he weren't a River, she'd be trying to peel them back like an onion.

"I'd like to start over," he said. "I'm going to be here for a week, and I hear you have some interesting ideas for the winery."

She tilted her chin. "Why would I tell you when you said you plan to sell? And I know it would be to some big corporation, which would most likely leave me without a job." While she trusted Weezer and believed that as long as the woman was in charge, Eliza Jane would be safe, she didn't trust that Malbec wouldn't be able to gain more control.

"For one, I know my mom made you some promises. And, secondly, I genuinely want to hear what you have in mind. Maybe we could brainstorm and come up with some better ideas."

Her eyes widened. All she could think about was how he could step in and take over.

That might be worse than a big-corporation buyout.

She swallowed. "Are you planning to come back?"

"Would you leave your job if you were me?"

She let out a short laugh. "I never would have taken a long-term job at that kind of vineyard." She held up her hand, cutting off his retort. "I know they make great wines. It's not about quality. It's about size. I don't want to be one of many. I want to be the one, and I don't mind being in a smaller setting to do that. It gives me more control, and the satisfaction is so much sweeter." She brought her fingers to her lips and sent a kiss out into the warm air. "I've turned around a few wineries that others had written off, and there is nothing better than watching that happen."

"If that's the case, why aren't you still doing that? Why stop here? Why make *this* your home?"

Those were valid questions. However, she wasn't sure how honest she wanted to be. Her father and grandfather used to talk about The River Winery when they were both near the end of their lives. They would discuss how pretty the land was. And when she pressed them on how well they knew it, they'd simply told her that they'd had the opportunity to visit once, and it had touched their soul like no other had.

Weezer had confirmed that story.

But Eliza Jane always found it odd that her father and grandfather never once drank the wine. It sat in their wine cooler with a big sign that read: *Do not drink.* She always thought that was odd because, while they were both wine snobs, they didn't have a bad thing to say about the River labels.

However, they really didn't have anything *good* to say about it either.

"I've enjoyed my work. I've learned a lot from every

winery I've ever worked at. But I want my own line, and I want to stay in one place. I want roots."

"I can understand that. I've planted my feet firmly in Napa." Malbec took her empty wrapper with his and stuffed them back into the small paper bag. "But my mom can't be the first person to offer you the chance to create your own brand name."

No way would she admit that he was correct with that point. She'd turned down two other offers, but for good reasons. The first one had been when her father was first diagnosed with cancer. The second time had been right after he died, and the gibberish that came out of her dad's mouth during his final days had made no sense. That said, he kept telling her that she needed to take back what was rightfully theirs. He kept saying that The River's Edge Winery had always been theirs.

Well, there was no such winery that she could ever find. The closest thing was The River Winery.

But the other strange thing her father had said the day he died had been that Weezer would understand. Oddly enough, two months later, Weezer showed up at Eliza Jane's front door. She'd once asked Weezer about her father and grandfather's trip to New Jersey, about that conversation. Weezer shrugged her shoulders and acted as if she hadn't a clue. She said she only remembered the two men because they were wine lovers and constantly talked about how beautiful and different the vineyard was compared to those in the west.

Which was true.

"Actually, she was," Eliza Jane lied. Her stomach churned. It wasn't something she was comfortable doing, and she could tell by the way Malbec smirked that he didn't believe her.

"All right. What kind of wine do you want to make?"

"I'd start with a heavy cabernet and nice crisp sauvignon blanc." She lifted her finger. "Under my name. But I'd to the River name a chardonnay. I think that is sorely lacking."

"Oaked or unoaked."

"Definitely oaked," she said with a bright smile. "And, to be honest, that's the first thing we should do. I've started a formula and…" She let her words trail off. Her excitement had gotten the better of her. Thus far, she'd only shared some of this with Weezer, and it would be a year or two before it came to market—if the blend were correct. Of course, they might have to buy some grapes from other vineyards until they could grow their own.

So many possibilities. But they had other challenges to deal with first. "But I'm getting way ahead of myself. I think the first two years, we need to deal with some rebranding of what we have already, and re-establish our reputation."

"It's interesting that you so easily use the pronoun *we* when talking about my family's business." He arched a brow.

She sucked in a deep breath and blinked. For

someone who wanted to start over, he was still acting like the enemy. "I'm a part of this winery now, whether you like it or not."

He tilted his head. "I suppose you are, but—"

"No. I am. There are no *buts* about it." Jumping to her feet, she wobbled. She flapped her hands like a wild bird and raised one of her legs in hopes of keeping her balance. It might be unseasonably warm outside, but that river was damn cold.

"Whoa there," he said as he managed to get to his feet, but that did neither of them any good as he toppled over into the water, taking her with him in a big splash.

She gasped as her skin hit the cold. Her peach sundress clung to her body—of all days not to wear a bra.

She slapped her hands at the surface, trying to swim for the dock, but the river took her a good ten feet south.

Malbec grasped her by the arm and tugged her to the bend in the river, helping her up onto the muddy bank. "Are you okay? You didn't hit any rocks, did you?" He held her by her forearms and looked her over. His gaze stopped at her nipples poking through the thin fabric of her clothing that acted as a second skin at this point.

"I'm fine." She shrugged from his embrace and crossed her arms over her chest. Thank goodness the cottage wasn't too far away. "You need to accept that this is your mother's winery. Not yours. And this is her decision." She turned on her heels and took two steps. She had half a mind to tell him all about the contract, but she'd yet to actually see it, much less sign it, and she didn't want to make matters worse.

He curled his fingers around her biceps and yanked her to his hard chest. "You fail to understand that this was a plan concocted by my mom to get me to return to Candlewood Falls and take my rightful place as the head of this winery. And if I decide to do that, she'll gladly turn the reins over to me, and what I say will be the final word." He heaved in a deep breath, pressing his body harder against hers. He wrapped his arms around her waist and licked his lips. His warm breath tickled her skin.

She couldn't move if she tried, but it was less because of his tight embrace and more about the way his eyes bored deep into her soul. The passion buried there spilled out into a fiery blaze that coated her wet skin like a warm towel.

"I've learned that Weezer doesn't *gladly* hand over control of anything to anyone. Not even the man she loves more than anything. So, I call that bullshit."

"Call it what you want, but my mother wants all her family back in Candlewood Falls, and she'll sell her soul to the devil to make that happen." He arched a brow. "You never want to underestimate Weezer. You'll lose your shirt."

Eliza Jane narrowed her eyes and heaved in a sharp

breath. Her lungs burned. She opened her mouth, but no words formed. She couldn't think of a single thing to say. He was right. Her fate hung in the wind and could be blown in any direction at any time. She felt confident that Weezer wanted her at the winery, but she wasn't entirely sure of Weezer's motives and that scared Eliza Jane.

"My mother won't go back on her word," Malbec said softly. His lips were way too close for comfort—plump and looking way too kissable. Too bad his personality tended to turn sour quickly. "She'll keep you on for as long as she has control."

"And what about you?"

If Malbec decided to come back before Eliza Jane could sign any contracts, things could drastically change for her, and she couldn't have that.

Nor could she afford to allow herself this flirtation.

He tilted his head and leaned a little closer. "I haven't decided yet." He brushed his lips gently over her mouth. It was soft and tender, and she reluctantly relaxed into his embrace. "It will all depend on the quality of your work and if I believe you add value to The River Winery."

She pressed her hand against the center of his chest and took a step back. Stiffening her spine and squaring her shoulders, she regained her composure. "I add a hell of a lot more worth than you do." She spun a hundred and eighty degrees and made a beeline for the cottage.

Malbec made her crazy. He was constantly picking fights with her and making her question her job security. She wanted him to leave Candlewood Falls and go back to Napa Valley.

But at the same time, she wanted him to stay. Part of her wanted to get to know the real Malbec because this brooding, moody man wasn't the person she saw hiding behind his kind and caring blue eyes. Inside his soul was a man with passion and vision. One that made her feel alive any time he touched her. And, deep down, she knew he wanted to come back. It frustrated her that she wanted to find out what held him back. To know what he was afraid of. It wasn't her business.

However, what was worse was her undeniable attraction to Malbec. Since the moment she'd laid eyes on him, she hadn't been able to stop thinking about him. But that was just his looks. Those meant nothing. She could see behind the handsome smile and sexy body to the tender man beneath, and she wanted to get to know him on all levels.

"Eliza Jane! Wait," Malbec called.

She didn't bother looking over her shoulder. "I need to change for work," she yelled as she turned the corner to the front of the cottage. "Besides, we're done talking." She stepped inside and slammed the door, leaning against it and closing her eyes. All she needed was for Malbec to go back to Napa Valley.

That would solve *all* her problems.

Or would it? Because she had to admit that despite

how much he frustrated her, he also made her feel alive in unexpected ways.

Malbec

"Fuck," Malbec mumbled. His baby sister had been partially right. At least, in this situation. He hadn't a clue how to relate to Eliza Jane because she had him all twisted up like a teenage boy with his first crush. He didn't know which end was up, and he was acting like a damn fool.

One second, he was being nice and kind.

And the next, he was acting like a jerk and trying to kiss her.

What a damn moron.

"Eliza Jane." He knocked on the door. "Let me in, please."

"I told you. I need to get changed for work."

He shoved his hands into his wet pockets, fingering his keys. No. That would be rude. Not to mention aggressive. And it could be considered breaking and entering since she was renting, and he wasn't the owner. "I want to apologize."

"Accepted."

He let out a long breath. "Can I at least borrow a towel to dry myself off a little? I believe I have a drawer of clothes from the last time I came home—"

"Fine." She yanked open the door. "But you're going to have to wait until after I change." She stomped off toward the dresser.

She opened a few drawers before rounding the corner into the bathroom. She shut the door harshly. The pictures on the wall rattled. He stood on the mat in the front of the cottage, dripping all over the place. The air-conditioning made him shiver.

For the first time in his adult life, he really had no clue what he wanted. Going back to Napa Valley seemed like something he wanted to put off. All of a sudden, his job felt less fulfilling. No. It wasn't the making of the wine because he loved every second of that. He enjoyed being out in the rolling hills and watching as the grapes ripened.

But he hadn't realized until this moment that he craved more. He needed to be challenged, and his career had become more of a gentle ride. Which wasn't necessarily bad. However, coming home, he'd realized that maybe some of what people had been saying about him was true.

He wasn't his mother, and the idea that he couldn't fill her shoes terrified him. He'd thought that if he went out into the world and proved himself, coming home would be easy.

However, the more he stayed away, the harder

moving back became, until he decided it wasn't an option.

Of course, there was also the stupid secret that his grandfather had made such a big deal about. He couldn't imagine what on Earth had his mother willing to put her family's life's work on the line, especially if it was something that went back generations. It made no sense.

Only, he suspected that all of their family's problems, including his parents' divorce, stemmed from whatever his grandfather had told his mom in private.

And then there was the sexy-ass woman in the bathroom. She scrambled his mind more than anything. He couldn't stand that the more Eliza Jane pushed, the more he wanted her. It wasn't normal. They acted like oil and water. If anyone listened in on their conversations, they would totally believe they disliked each other.

Maybe she couldn't stand him, but he found her utterly fascinating. She was witty, intelligent, and well-spoken. Well, that was until she got her tail feathers all ruffled.

Hell, he kind of liked that.

Shit. There really was something wrong with him. Maybe he should ask one of his sisters—though definitely not Zinfandel—for advice on women. Maybe Chablis or Riesling. They were much more refined and didn't think putting a vibrator on full blast in a bag and sending it through security only to watch the TSA person grab it while searching was funny.

Okay. So maybe it was sort of hysterical, but still. Taking direction about how to get Eliza Jane to warm up to him from a twenty-two-year-old wasn't a good idea. But the real question was, why did he need to get close to Eliza Jane? Was it because he let his baby sister push his buttons? Or because he wanted to know if she was good for the winery and he could leave, knowing it would be well taken care of? Or was it something else?

It was that last question that left him feeling totally out of his comfort zone. For his entire adult life, he'd been in charge of his destiny. He'd had a plan and executed it.

Eliza Jane put a big ol' wrench in that well-thought-out road to what he imagined was success.

Selling the winery was still very much on the table, depending on what his mother's real plans for the future were. Bringing in a stranger was one thing, but what about when his mother was actually too old to make decisions? If Malbec didn't come home, they'd still be left with having to sell.

The bathroom door flung open, and Eliza Jane stepped out wearing a pair of capri jeans and a light blue shirt. "The bathroom is all yours. The clothes you left are in the trunk over there." She pointed to some storage bins stacked in the corner. "Your mom was going to pick them up this week and take them to her place."

"I see." He strolled across the room. His mom had really meant business when she'd brought Eliza Jane to the winery. "Thanks." He snagged some shorts and a long-sleeved shirt. "Would you mind locking up after I leave?"

"Please, don't go." He held open the bathroom door and caught her gaze. "We need to find some common ground here."

"Why?"

He raked a hand through his wet hair. "Because this is my family's business, and my mom doesn't want to sell it to a big corporation. She wants me home. And, maybe this is where I belong."

"You've got to be kidding me." Eliza Jane planted her hands on her hips. "You're that threatened by me?"

"No. It has nothing to do with that," he said as calmly as he could.

"Well, it certainly feels that way, and you have to realize that this decision doesn't bode well for me."

"Me coming back is better than us selling and new management having no use for you or your line at all, so let's look at the brighter side of things."

"Come on. You've made it clear how you feel about my presence here. Something about evaluating my worth."

"Okay. So bad choice of words."

"Get real. This place isn't big enough for your ego, much less both of ours."

He tossed his head back and laughed. "I'm not that conceited."

"Oh, yes, you are."

"Okay. If we're pointing out shortcomings, you're more stubborn than ten of my mom."

"I wouldn't go that far, but I'm not going to argue," she said. "Why did you change your mind all of a sudden? If I don't threaten you, there has to be a reason. What is it?"

Wow. She certainly knew how to pivot a conversation quickly. He rubbed his neck, feeling as though she'd just given him whiplash. He cleared his throat. "Let me get out of these wet clothes and we can take a stroll toward the main building. I'll tell you why I'm considering having a hand in running the winery and what that might look like."

"Fine," she said. "You have from here to the gift shop to explain yourself."

"Perfect." He stepped into the bathroom and shed his wet clothes. He wished he had a fully formed answered. Right now, all he had were a couple of strange feelings that he didn't quite understand, and a few points laid out by his siblings.

That wasn't good enough.

And how did he anticipate approaching his employer on how he'd do both? That would be interesting.

He needed a plan. And a good one. Not just something he told Eliza Jane to calm her nerves so they could work together for the next week as he figured it all out. A real, bona fide proposal for the future of The River Winery and both their roles.

That was if he decided that selling wasn't the best plan.

Shit. His stomach twisted into a million knots. He had no idea what was best, except that he knew, without a doubt, that he couldn't leave without hearing every single idea Eliza Jane had, and giving all of this more than a good mulling over.

He had to come up with something that made sense now, or he'd blow any chance he had to earn her trust. And he knew he needed it because his mother wasn't going to let her go, and Eliza Jane wanted to stay. If he had any chance of having the best of both worlds, Eliza Jane had to continue on.

But he also needed his siblings. The winery should have a next generation. They had to agree that they would step up. If they weren't all in, there was no point.

He hiked up his shorts and pulled the shirt over his head. He decided to leave his wet pieces of fabric hanging in the shower. She could return them later, or he'd come and pick them up tomorrow. He stepped into the main room where she stood with a couple of mugs of coffee.

"I thought you might be a little chilled."

"I am, but I need the caffeine more." He took the much-needed jolt and headed toward the front door where he opened it and let her walk through first. He twisted the lock and closed it. "Hey, slow down. I need to talk to you, and you're not giving me a fair shake."

She let out a long sigh. "I don't trust you," she blurted out. "Ever since you got here, things have been weird for me. All I want to do is turn this place around and make really good wine."

"That's all I want to do, too."

She stopped dead in her tracks and glared. "No. You came here to sell this place to some big corporation—who will do a great job, I'm sure. But they won't have much use for me or my old-fashioned ways. Nor will they let me have a line. They will change everything about The River Winery. They might even change the name. I get that I just got here, and there is no reason for you or anyone, including Weezer, to give a shit about me, but I can't believe you're just going to let four generations disappear into obscurity. And, trust me, your family history will disappear into the walls. In five to ten years, no one will even know who Weezer River was."

"That's impossible. Especially in this town."

"You think that's true. But, eventually, people will stop talking about her and the River family because whoever buys the vineyard will rewrite the narrative. And don't you dare tell me it will be different. The vineyard you work for is grappling with that right now. That family is being written right out of their own history."

He knew that all of that was true, but he wasn't about to admit it out loud. Part of him really liked the idea of selling and how it would give his parents some enormous freedoms. Not to mention, his siblings could go and do whatever they wanted.

But that wasn't the message he was getting.

From anyone in his family. And that was the reality he needed to deal with.

"You have to understand that my mother had me believing she had a buyer. It's not like I brought one to her feet."

"But you went and found one as soon as you got here, and you've wanted her to sell for the last five years. You've been begging her to consider it."

He raised his hands to the sky. "That's not entirely true. And you don't know the entire story between me and Mom."

"Oh. She's told me why, and it's a lame excuse."

He waggled his finger. "I know my mother. There is no way in hell she told you the entire story of why I refused to come back and help with the family business. Or even why I now believe it's time to let it go."

She opened her mouth, but he didn't give her a chance to say a single word. He'd had enough.

"Did you ever wonder why I'm the only one who went into the business of grape-growing or winemaking?"

Her jaw dropped open as she nodded.

"Did you know that my sister Chablis has the same

degree I do, but after she saw what I was going through, she ran off and became a firefighter? And my brother, Merlot, started off in the same program, but quickly changed his second year and became a parole officer."

"Those are two quite different careers," Eliza Jane said softly.

Malbec let out a slight chuckle. "The only reason the three youngest are even remotely in the business is because as much as we tried to shield them from the insanity that is my mother, they grew up in a very different environment and didn't see some of the weird things the rest of us did as kids."

"I don't think Weezer is any different than the rest of us. Misunderstood maybe, but that's about it."

"That's true," Malbec said. "But growing up as her kid wasn't easy. My mom has softened a lot in her old age. People in this town aren't as afraid of her as they used to be. However, that doesn't change the fact that one of my friends in grammar school told me that he couldn't come over and play because someone told his mom that my mom had loaded shotguns in the house and often threatened to use them if anyone behaved badly."

"Oh. That's horrible. I hope it wasn't true."

Malbec smacked his forehead. "Well, not really. I mean, we have guns, sure, but they aren't loaded. They are locked in a gun closet, and the ammunition is secured in a different cabinet. And my mom doesn't threaten children. Just adults. But she doesn't mean it. And of course, she once said she was going to go after one of the alpacas that came onto the vineyard. They were eating some of our best grapes. She was pissed. But she's like madly in love with the stupid creatures now. She pretends she's not, but she totally loves the one named Alpacino. Has for years. And she keeps opening the fence and letting them in. I swear she feeds them on purpose."

"So I've heard," Eliza Jane muttered. "And I've seen the evidence. There are fresh vegetables and fruits at the property line every day. I think that's how she keeps them off the land, even though she encourages them."

"That and the fact that she ropes off the fence and only lets them into the vineyard when it serves her purposes." Malbec shook his head. "That should tell you that she loves the alpacas and uses them when she wants. And, trust me, my mother has a reason for everything. We might not get it, but it makes perfect sense to her."

Eliza Jane continued down the path toward the main building as it wove through the vineyard. "Why do you think your mother came looking for me and offered me this job?"

"My mom has always kept a finger on the pulse of this business. I suspect she believes you're really good at your job," Malbec admitted. "But I don't know why you're so important to her on a personal level, and that is something I want to find out." Gently, he curled his fingers around her forearm, forcing her to stop. He turned her body and stared deep into her eyes. "When my grandfather died, he told me there was a secret. One that would change the course of my life."

"What kind of secret?"

"It has something to do with this winery and the land it sits on. My grandfather said a lot of strange things before he died, but the weirdest was that it was up to me to toe the line and make sure the secret stayed buried just like his father and he had done, and Mom did after. He wouldn't tell me what it was. Said that had to come from my mother. That it was tradition. But when he got sick, he said even stranger things. Stuff that made no sense. But now I wonder if perhaps I should have been paying more attention. And what really bothers me is that my mom refuses to tell me the secret. She said it was a burden that'd nearly destroyed her relationship with her father, and one I didn't need. Ironically, that damn secret has come between my parents and me in more ways than one. My grandfather told my mom it was the only way to keep the winery at its best. I told my mom that if she couldn't tell me what Grandpa was talking about, then I'd never come home and run it."

Eliza Jane tilted her head. "My grandfather also said some strange things right before he died. And, oddly, some of them had to do with his trip to this winery."

"Why do you think that was?" Malbec scratched the

back of his neck. "Your grandfather was a lawyer, right? He wasn't in the wine business."

"He never finished law school," she said. "My father and grandfather sold wine, much like your siblings do, and had a specialty shop. But my great-grandfather worked at wineries, and there are stories that he owned a winery at one point."

Malbec pressed his hand to the small of her back and guided her along the path toward the main building. "Where in the country was the winery he owned?"

"That is a bit of a mystery," she said. "And it was always a sore subject with my grandpa. To the point he wouldn't even discuss it, other than to say that his dad gambled away anything and everything important. So, I never pushed. I did, however, try to get my dad to open up about it, but he told me he didn't know."

"Did you believe him?"

"Not one bit," she admitted. "My father and grandpa are as thick as thieves."

"Sounds like both our families enjoy secrets." Malbec was generally interested in Eliza Jane's family's history. Because he wanted to know more about her and her life. But he needed to first deal with his mother and whatever haunted *her* past. He needed his mom to share about the history of the vineyard so he could best make decisions about his future and that of The River Winery. Once he did that, he could then explore the feelings that circled his heart when it came to Eliza Jane.

Because all he wanted to do was kiss her again.

Actually, he wanted a lot more.

"What are you doing for dinner tonight?" He stood in front of the main doors at the gift shop.

She shrugged. "I haven't given it much thought.

"I'd like to take you out. There's a great restaurant just outside of town. My treat. We can talk about plans for the winery."

"You haven't really given me a strong reason to tell you anything."

He laughed. "I want to hold onto my shares of The River Winery and continue working in Napa Valley." He pressed his finger over her lips. "As long as my mom is willing to step down, and your plans are in line with mine and you're willing to work with me, I think we could have the best of all worlds."

She furrowed her brow. "But that means I'm never an owner."

"Probably not," he said. "I and my siblings would still own the winery, but you'd have your own line, and you'd have control of that as well as management and a lifelong position. Isn't that what you want?"

"I do want that." She tucked her hair behind her ears.

He wanted to twist those strands between his fingers.

"But I also wanted a percentage."

"I'm willing to give you that in your line, but not in the winery. It's already going to be split eight ways between my siblings, me, and my parents—for as long as they are alive."

"I have to think about that. Getting skin in the game so I'm never pushed out was something I needed in the employment contract with your mom."

"If I take over, and my siblings are with me, I'm not sure that's going to happen," he said. "I will talk with them, but why don't we have dinner to hash it all out?"

"We just did." She pushed open the door.

He blinked. That wasn't what he'd had in mind. Or what he'd expected her to say to his proposal. "Um. Well. I think we still have some things to discuss."

"Are you good with a grill?"

"As long as it's steak."

"Perfect. Pick up a couple and a bottle of wine and I'll make a salad. I'll see you at seven." She slipped through the door into the gift shop of the winery, leaving him standing outside.

Well, that settled that. Now, he had some shopping to do, not to mention he needed to find his mother. She had some explaining to do. And this time, he wasn't going to take her standard answers.

8

———

WEEZER

"**W**hatcha doing, old man?" Weezer set some grapes and other treats on the ground for Alpacino. She perched herself on a large rock by the hole in the fence between the winery and the alpaca farm.

Alpacino cocked his head and smiled.

Well, Weezer *thought* he smiled. Then he lowered his head and chomped on the food.

"You the only one in this town besides Carter who understands me. And even he doesn't get it sometimes."

"I take offense to that," a familiar voice rang out.

Weezer jerked. "Damn. You scared me." She patted her chest.

Carter leaned against the post. "I thought I might find you out here." He glanced at the animal. "I'm surprised you don't have a bag packed and aren't running off with this sexy creature."

Weezer laughed. "Don't tempt me." She pulled the piece of paper from her pocket. Normally, she kept it in the safe in Carter's closet. It was the one place the kids wouldn't look for any secrets—not that they knew what they'd be looking for.

"Funny you should be carrying that thing around." He pointed. "It's exactly what I wanted to talk to you about."

"I can't tell them," she said, shaking her head. Her heart hurt so much, she thought it might burst. She wanted to hate her grandfather and father for doing this to her and her children. It had been the worst burden to carry, and she would not pass it down to her kids. "Our children and Eliza Jane can never know what my grandfather did. I can make this right without them ever knowing the truth."

"But the truth will set you free." Carter inched closer. He tapped her thigh and sat down on the rock next to her. Birds chirped overhead. Alpacino just stared at them with oddly kind eyes.

"You need to have more faith in our children and their ability to forgive. Besides, it won't change anything, and God only knows what other secrets are buried in this land. Your father always loved to talk about a box of buried secrets that he wished he could find because he'd like to burn it."

"I used to have to send you out in the middle of the night because he'd go digging for it." She reached into her other pocket and pulled out another piece of paper —the one she'd never shown Carter.

The one she'd hidden in various places inside her home throughout her entire life.

The one that would destroy her family if Eliza Jane ever got her hands on it.

The one that proved there *were* other secrets. God forbid anyone ever find that box. She had no clue what was in it—though her father did say that even he wasn't entirely sure what was in the container. Only that he knew of its existence.

Weezer handed the paper to Carter with a shaky hand. "My dad gave this to me a few months after Riesling was born."

Carter shifted his gaze between the paper and her. "We got divorced about that time." He waved the document under her nose. "Is this why you decided we could no longer be married? That I shouldn't be part-owner of the winery, at least on paper?"

Weezer wiped the tears that escaped her eyes. Typically, she wasn't the type of person who cried in front of other people—not even the man she loved the most in this world.

But this was a unique situation. Her entire life had been wrapped up in a lie. Everything she'd done hadn't been about protecting the lie but making sure her family wasn't hurt by it any more than necessary. If they had found out the truth about how her grandfather had acquired the winery, it would have been devastating.

But knowing that she'd perpetuated it by having the knowledge that there was a living relative who was the rightful owner?

Her kids would never forgive her.

Perhaps that's why she pushed them all away. But the one thing she couldn't answer was why she'd never been willing to sell. Had she done that, this would have never been a problem. Of course, her family would have had to leave Candlewood Falls for good.

"Yes," she whispered.

"My God," Carter said. "This is a confession from your grandfather, stating he didn't win the winery. He stole it from Elijah James 'EJ' Blue. He cheated a man out of his family business and called it his." Carter slumped forward. "You didn't know about this until after Riesling was born?"

"I swear, I didn't."

"Did your father know?"

"He swore to me that he didn't know until the winery was in my name."

"Shit, Weezer. That was when Chablis was born." Carter ran a hand over the top of his head. "Why the hell did that old coot feel the need to fucking confess."

"I don't know," Weezer admitted. "But I wish my father never felt the need to tell me."

"No wonder you were such a mess when Eliza's dad and grandpa blew through town."

"I thought for sure they were going to tell me they'd filed some legal proceedings to take the winery away from us. That's when I knew I needed to find a way to merge our families. I just wasn't sure how to do it, and it couldn't be with joining forces with either of them."

"I did find it odd how hostile they acted toward you. Did they always know the winery was stolen?"

She let out a slight chuckle. "No. At least not from what I could tell. We never talked about it. They just made strange, all-knowing comments about gambling and taking advantage of people, and then they left. I never heard from them again. But I kept my eye on them and their little shop."

"I'm sure you did," Carter said.

"I don't want this for our children. But knowing that Eliza Jane, who was named after her great-grandfather, was out there and wanting to make wine… couldn't let that go. I had to bring her here, and I needed to know her. The second I met her and saw she was perfect for Malbec, I thought maybe this was the answer to making all these wrongs one big right. But I couldn't just go and put her in our will."

"No. You couldn't do that without causing a ruckus." Carter put a strong arm around her shoulders and pulled her close. "You can't meddle in Malbec's life." He kissed her temple. "If he's going to fall in love and get married, that has to be on his terms. But I understand better now why you've done certain things."

She blinked, glancing up. "You're not insanely mad?"

"I never said that." He gave her a good squeeze. "You should never have kept this from me, and us getting a divorce was never the answer. But what's done is done. The question is, how do we proceed?"

"You can't tell them."

Carter swiped his thumb and forefinger across his square chin.

"You know I'm right."

"No. I just don't believe we can throw it all at them at once. I'm trying to figure out the best plan of action. And, also, we have to consider how Eliza Jane will take to all of this. And then there are the legalities of it—*if* this is true." He waved the paper. "Something I need to do some research on."

"Do you think it's possible that my grandfather was just speaking gibberish?"

"Anything's possible. Why don't you let me do some digging, and we can just sit on this for a bit?"

"We can't afford to let Malbec go back to Napa Valley. He has to stay."

"Even if he does decide that he wants to return to Candlewood Falls and The River Winery, he'll have to return to California for a bit to leave his job properly and pack his belongings. Let's focus on finding out as much of the truth as we can. I know he's already talked to the twins and Zinfandel about what it would look like if he kept a finger on the pulse but still lived in Napa."

"That's not a good idea."

"Maybe not. But he's thinking about being involved, and that's a start."

"Yeah. However, once we tell him what my grandfather did, he won't want a damn thing to do with this winery, and we'll have to give it all lock, stock, and barrel to Eliza Jane anyway. Not that I don't want her to have it, because that's why I brought her here, but I also still want to keep it in our family. My grandfather might have stolen it, but the rest of us put our blood, sweat, and tears into this place."

"I understand," Carter said. "How long have you been planning this little matchmaking scheme of yours?"

"Honestly, I've been cooking it up for about two years. But Faith really made me think it could work when she had that vision or whatever it was. Not that I believe in them, but she just moved here. What the hell does she know?"

"Enough. Her family has been here forever." Carter sucked in a deep breath. "You have to promise me that from here on in, we have no more secrets. And that you will let me handle all this—including Eliza Jane's contract."

"She wants a percentage, and she wants it so if we

ever *do* sell, she's as much of an owner as the kids—though a smaller piece of the pie." Weezer arched a brow. "Those were her numbers. I would split it equally among them all."

"This is a screwed-up situation. It will eventually come out."

She nodded. Carter was right. But they had to somehow control the how and when. "Do you remember the week before my grandfather died and all the crazy things he said?"

"I do." Carter tilted his head. "Are you thinking there's really a box of secrets out by the river's edge?"

"My grandfather was a strange, old man."

"Agreed." Carter let out a slight chuckle. "Well, maybe we should go digging? And before I forget, I heard through the grapevine that Malbec and Eliza Jane are having dinner tonight." He pushed himself from the rock, taking Weezer into his arms. "I have to admit, I do think you might be right about those two."

"I know I am. But our son is too much like me. Now that he knows what I planned, he'll never even consider it."

"You're not giving our son enough credit." Carter pushed her hair over her shoulders. "Since you're backing off, he's going to be curious. That's his nature, and we raised him to be that way."

The corners of her mouth curved into an upward smile. "When all of this is over, I just might have to marry you again."

. . .

Malbec

Malbec closed the back door of his vehicle and heard the sound of some Southern rock song coming from the back patio. He took his bag of groceries and two bottles of his signature wine and strolled around the side of the cottage. He leaned against the wood railing and stared at the sexy woman doing a little dance while watering some plants. Her backside wiggled back and forth to the beat of the drums.

As quietly as he could, he set the bag on the table. He didn't want to startle her and have her turn, spraying him with water. He cleared his throat as soon as he thought he was out of spraying distance. "Hey there," he said.

She spun on her heels. "Hey yourself." She twisted the nozzle and coiled the hose. "You're a few minutes early."

"It's a River curse." He lifted the top to the grill and cringed. It would take a good ten minutes to burn off the crud that had collected on the grate. He turned the switch and lit one of the burners.

And then the second and third.

"What are you doing?" she asked. "Are you ready to grill?"

"This thing is disgusting. I wouldn't eat off it." He pointed.

She placed her hand on his shoulder and leaned over. "Gross. I've never used it. Your mom said she had someone put in a new tank. I assumed it would be clean."

"Never assume anything when it comes to my mom. She generally takes care of everything, but something always slips through the cracks. Seems that this is one of those things. The good news is that it's not that difficult to take care of, and by the time it burns off, I'll be ready to cook the steaks. They have been marinating for the last few hours. I also brought some corn."

"Sounds great." She pulled out a bottle of wine. "Shall I open this?"

"Please. By all means. I brought it for us to enjoy."

She glanced at the label. "Oh. This looks like a good year."

"One of our finest." He closed the top of the grill. "We should really work toward recreating this blend and flavor."

"We? You say that as if you've made up your mind." She stood at the outside bar and uncorked the bottle. She put an aerator into the top before pouring two glasses and handing him one, giving him a chance to mull over his answer, which was a complicated one.

His current employer understood he had ownership in his family winery. When he negotiated the contract, he'd made sure that wouldn't be a problem in case,

God forbid, something happened to his parents, and he was left with the business and had to do something with it. He certainly didn't want a conflict of interest.

Now, all he had in his heart and mind was conflict, and he had no clue what to do. He couldn't talk to his mom because she wanted him to hook up with Eliza Jane.

No way would Malbec have a conversation with his father about it, because he always took his mom's side.

His brothers were useless and would only either end up giving him a hard time or feeding him stupid ideas that would only scare Eliza Jane away. Talking to his sisters might give him some useful information, but they couldn't keep their mouths shut to save their sorry collective asses.

"I honestly haven't," he said. Giving Eliza Jane a line of crap or a contrived answer would only make matters worse. "This is the first time since I graduated college that I've given coming back to Candlewood Falls any serious thought. I still prefer the idea of having the best of both worlds."

"That's a lot on one man's plate." She pulled out a chair and made herself comfortable at the table. She'd already set it and put a large salad bowl with plastic wrap pulled tightly over the top in the center.

His mother would be impressed. Weezer liked to be prepared.

He took a step back and examined the cottage. It needed a fresh coat of paint and, at first glance, appeared to be run-down and in need of a ton of repairs. But when he looked closely at what he thought were major problems, he found that they were easy fixes. He had to wonder how far his mother had gone to make it look as if the winery were slipping through her fingers, because there was nothing wrong with the vineyard. The grapes were in perfect condition.

So, why had the last two years of wine tasted off?

Because his mother wanted it to.

She'd stop at nothing to get her way.

Now he had to ask why she had given up so quickly and agreed to have a real discussion with him about the future.

"I've worked hard to get where I am. I'm not inclined to give it up so easily." He picked up the scraper and rubbed it over the grill. "However, since I've been home, I've really paid attention to how much my mom and the rest of my family needs me."

"Are you doing this out of guilt?"

"I haven't done anything yet. And, no." He pulled the steaks out of the bag and opened the container. After tossing them onto the grill, he added the foiled-wrapped corn. Dinner would be ready in about ten minutes. He enjoyed that they could converse while he cooked. It gave him something mindless to do as he searched for the right thing to say.

Which seemed to be the truth—even when he wasn't exactly sure what that was.

"I've never felt guilty for leaving. Or staying away," he admitted.

"Did you get a chance to ask your mom about that secret?"

He shook his head. "I'm going to be spending some time with her tomorrow. I'll do it then."

"Is that really the reason you refused to come home and work at the winery all these years?" She lifted the glass to her lips and took a slow slip.

He tried desperately not to stare, but that became impossible. "When my grandfather told me there was a secret, my mother went off on him like I'd never seen before. And trust me when I say that Weezer River didn't argue with her father, much less speak back to him, but she cursed him out like a drunken sailor."

And in front of a few of her older kids.

When the fight concluded, his mom told him that he was never to speak of it to his grandfather again. That his grandpa had misspoken and that his mind was fractured.

"Older generations are so weird when it comes to grudges and secrets. It drove me nuts. When my grandpa found out that his father used to own a winery and never told anyone, and then refused to discuss where it was or why he'd let it go, it caused a rift. I believe my father and grandfather found out what happened to that winery because that rift became loathing."

Malbec poked the steaks and flipped them. The

smell of fresh, cooking meat hit his nostrils, making his stomach growl. "They never told you?"

"Whatever winery he owned, he lost it in a card game. I guess he had a drinking and gambling problem. My grandfather blamed him for my grandma running out on them and the fact they were always poor. I think learning there had been a family business and that he'd gambled it away about killed both my father and grandfather."

"That's really rough."

"I have to admit, I'm a little jealous that your secrets don't really affect your family relationships."

He tossed his head back and laughed. It wasn't a real one, but more of a fake, sarcastic one. "Are you kidding me? We're crazy dysfunctional. I'd say the only difference is that we're not willing to cut each other out of our lives completely. But we've all set up boundaries and occasionally have to remind each other of them."

"The only thing that secret might have done is keep you from being where you belong. But I suspect there is more to that story than meets the eye."

"I don't know about that." He turned the corn and closed the lid. Only about three more minutes before he'd be slapping that perfectly cooked meat on their plates.

"I can understand you getting upset, but for over fifteen years? Something else must have happened."

Malbec hated to admit, even to himself, that Eliza Jane was right. This was a threefold story. The first part being the secret he didn't know. The second part being how his mother never quite trusted him to actually oversee the production of the wine.

But the final kicker had been two years ago when his mother had scared off the one woman he'd had any real feelings for. Her only excuse had been that he'd thank her later.

Right. That day would never come.

He'd forgiven his mother, and that girl had moved on. She was actually engaged to be married, and Malbec did his best to be happy for her and her new fiancé. What choice did he have?

"Lots of things have happened, but it's the secret that has kept me from wanting to run the family business. It's what kept the rest of my siblings from wanting it, as well."

"So, they all know there is a big, dark past?"

Malbec nodded. "The twins and Zinfandel don't care. They figure the past is in the past. Chablis wants nothing to do with the winery, but she's still hurt. So is Merlot. Riesling struggles the most with her relationship with my mom."

"Even more than you?"

"Oh, yeah. But that has less to do with the secret and more to do with Riesling's ex and how that affects my niece, Ashling."

"I got to meet her this morning when Riesling stopped by with something for your dad. It was in passing and really short, but she seems like such a sweet and smart little girl."

"That she is. But when my mom has an opinion about the person you date and it's not a good one, beware. Well, my mother hated Theo with a passion and made that poor man's life miserable."

"Weezer told me he was a deadbeat and that he hasn't seen his daughter in almost two years."

"That's only partly true," Malbec said. "Theo is a jerk. And he's a shitty father. But he's not required to send child support, and if they'd been married, my sister would have been the one paying *him* alimony."

"Your mom made it sound like Ashling's dad does nothing."

"Well, he doesn't come around, that's for sure." He flipped open the grill and stabbed the steaks. They were perfect. He placed them on the plates with the corn and set them on the table before topping off the wine and joining Eliza Jane. "Thing is, when he does show up, Ashling lights up like a Christmas tree. She doesn't know anything other than he's her father and she loves him. Only he doesn't come here to see her. He comes for a handout, and my sister often gives it to him because it's easier than breaking her daughter's heart."

"That's a shitty position to be in."

"It is. We all wish it were different, and my mom always tries to cut Theo off at the pass when he shows up in town, but again, once Ashling sees him, we all just have to sit back and let it play out."

"Did you ever think you are all doing exactly what your mom has been doing with that secret? What my great-grandpa did when he gambled away his winery and didn't tell his family? That maybe, in the long run, not telling her the truth about her father will only hurt her more?"

"She's too young to understand all that right now."

Eliza Jane tilted her head. "The longer you perpetuate this, the harder it will become to tell the truth. Just like it was for our parents."

Malbec had to admit that she had a valid point. One that made way too much sense. However, it wasn't his place to tell his sister what to do. And then there was his mother. The puppet master.

Maybe during their conversation tomorrow, he'd broach the topic. Why the hell not? It was time that things changed around here.

"You're a very wise woman, Eliza Jane." He tipped his glass. "Cheers to what I hope will be a great friendship."

She tapped her glass against his and took a large sip before picking up her knife and fork and slicing into the tender steak.

He leaned back in his chair and soaked up the pretty view. He hadn't been this enamored by a lady in a long time, and he wasn't sure how to handle it. Eliza Jane wasn't the kind of woman he would ever want a one-night stand with. He respected her too much, and he also knew he'd want more.

And it wasn't about sex.

It was about being in her company. He hung on her every word and genuinely valued her opinions, even when they disagreed. He wanted to hear what she had to say on any and every subject.

She waved her fork. "Oh, my God. This is delicious."

"Thank you. I made the marinade myself."

"I can taste the family wine." She nodded. "Your father makes this, doesn't he? We sell this."

"We do. But I made it fresh and, of course, the steaks have to be cooked properly."

"Well, hats off to the chef." She rolled her corn into the butter palette. Some dribbled down her chin when she took a few bites off the cob.

He reached across the table and dabbed at her face with a napkin.

"Thank you." She blinked a few times.

A sudden quietness came over them as they finished the last few nibbles of their meals. He stared out at the sun as it kissed the horizon, casting a glow over the vineyards. It wasn't the rolling hilltops of Napa Valley, but nothing was more magical than Candlewood Falls and the small river that ran through the winery. When he was a kid, he'd found an old black-and-white picture of three rows of grapevines. In front of them was a sign that read *The River's Edge*. When he asked his parents, they told him that his great-grandfather had originally named the winery that when he was still doing moonshine, but when they went legit, they changed the name.

Later, he'd looked it up in the history books in the library and, sure enough, the original name had been, *The River's Edge.*

The River Winery made much more sense since their main product became wine, not whiskey.

"I love sitting out here at night," she said softly.

"How long have you been in Candlewood Falls?"

"A little over a week," she admitted. "I never thought New Jersey could be so beautiful. I expected to be staring at skyscrapers or sandwiched houses on an overcrowded beach."

He laughed as he tossed his napkin onto his empty plate. "Oh. We have those too, but this is the part of New Jersey that people forget exists, and we're all sorts of secretly happy about that. Except for when they show up to buy our wine and spend their money in our town."

"You sound like you miss it."

"I do." He stood, piling the dirty dishes on top of one another. "I miss the change of seasons, and I miss my family."

"I appreciate you being honest with me about that." She followed him into the kitchen with the rest of the table settings.

They settled in next to one another in front of the sink and seamlessly worked to tackle the dirty dishes. It was an odd feeling to be elbow-to-elbow with her, and while there was definitely a fair amount of tension, it wasn't the kind of conflict that his presence at the winery had created.

This had a much more personal flare, and he found himself inching closer until his forearm touched hers.

"So, be truthful with me about where you see my role here at the winery," she said.

"Thus far, you appear to be as good as my mother says you are. So, if I choose to stay in Napa Valley, I would think you'd manage and oversee everything while answering to my mother and me. And, eventually, if I can talk Merlot and Chablis into it, they would play a more active role in the daily functions—though it's possible, if I stay on, they might want to give up their current careers."

"That means there's a possibility that you would quit your job and come back here." She turned and leaned her hip against the counter. "That would displace me."

He wiped his hand on the towel and set it on top of the drying rack. "I don't want that to happen." Resting his hands gently on her hips, he inched closer. "No matter what I do, I want to keep you on."

"Why? Because just a day ago—"

"Tonight's dinner is about starting over, and I told you, you're good at your job."

"No. You said it *appeared* that I was. Is there really room for the two of us here?" She held his glare with an unblinking stare.

"There's room for you and my mom. Why wouldn't there be room for you and me?"

"That's different, and you know it. She's a master. I'm still learning."

He circled his arms around her waist, heaving her to his chest. "Do not sell yourself that short. You're incredible, and you are no more of an apprentice to my mother than I am."

"It's still different because she's not going to be here for as long as I am. You and I are about the same age." She rested her hands on his shoulders and tilted her head. "I've already seen how we might butt heads on some procedures."

"I can be open-minded."

"Not when it comes to making your family wine." She licked her lips, which were the color of a rose. "I know I sound like a broken record, but I can't put in any more time here if I'm going to be pushed out in five years."

"That's bullshit."

She narrowed her eyes. "Why would you say that?"

"Because you have the chance to make your own line. Very few wineries will help you fund that."

"If I ever leave, I'll have to leave that behind, too. And how can I trust that, in five or ten years from now, you won't sell The River Winery, along with my hard work."

"That's a risk you'll need to be willing to take if you want your own label that badly," he said. "You've got a lot more opportunities here than you would anywhere else. You can go really far." His heart swelled with pride for what his family had created. And, damn, he was so proud to be a part of it.

Even from a distance.

He leaned closer until his lips were less than an inch from hers. "I better get going," he whispered. "It's getting late." He covered her mouth with his in a soft and tender yet unexpected kiss that he let linger.

She let out a soft moan as her fingers dug into his shoulders. Their tongues swirled and twisted around each other in a hot, seductive dance that needed no music.

Even though he didn't want to, he pulled back. "I'll see you at the office tomorrow."

"I guess you will."

He brushed his lips over hers one more time, letting them linger a little longer than appropriate. He groaned. "You're a dangerous woman."

"Why do you say that?"

"Because you're the kind of person I could absolutely fall for."

She took him by the hand and led him across the only room in the cottage.

He became painfully aware of the queen-sized bed in the corner.

"But that is the last time you're ever going to kiss me." She opened the door. "You might be attractive, but you're definitely not the kind of man I would ever become involved with." She pushed him out the door, closed it, and clicked the lock.

"Damn, that really bruised my ego," he mumbled as he made his way to his car, glancing over his shoulder. That wasn't how he'd expected the evening to end. And now he'd have to find a way to redeem himself.

Again.

9

ELIZA JANE

Eliza Jane took the mirror that Jenna handed to her and checked out the back of her hair. She'd never had highlights before, and she hated to admit that she loved them. "This looks amazing," she said.

"I'm so glad you like it."

"This is going to sound like a silly question, but how often do I have to come back and do this?"

"I'd say every three to four months. We don't want to overdo the highlights, but we will need to deal with the regrowth. So, why don't you make an appointment for a cut and color in three months, and we can see how your hair grows and make adjustments from there."

"Sounds great. Thanks."

Jenna ran her fingers through Eliza Jane's hair a few more times, adjusting it to her liking. "What's it like working for Weezer?"

"So far, she's great."

"I do her hair, and I have to admit, I was terrified the first few times. She can be a tough nut. But deep down, she's a kind person."

"I've seen a real tender side to her when it comes to her kids," Eliza Jane said. "What do you know about the history of the winery? Like how the River family came into the land to start it?" Shit. Eliza Jane really needed to stop diving right into conversations that could be considered weird.

"I really don't know," Jenna said. "There is a book in the library about the history of Candlewood Falls. It talks about all the original businesses and founders of the town. I'm sure there's something about the winery in there." Jenna wiped Eliza Jane's shoulders and took off the protective cape. "Or you could just ask Weezer. She's full of stories. If you want to know the truth about anything, she's the person to ask. If it's not true, she won't repeat it." Jenna leaned closer. "But she can also be secretive. If she doesn't want you to know something, she can be tight-lipped. I've heard that's why Malbec hasn't come home to run the winery. But that's something that Weezer doesn't talk about, and she's very proud of Malbec. She's proud of all her kids, though I sometimes think she has a weird way of showing it to them."

"I've gotten that impression." Eliza Jane slipped from the chair and followed Jenna to the front desk.

"It was a pleasure meeting you," Jenna said. "Hopefully, I'll see you around town or maybe we can get a cup of coffee sometime."

"I'd like that." Eliza Jane took care of the tip and made an appointment for her next cut and color. She stepped out of the beauty salon feeling as though she'd been super self-indulgent. She hadn't had that much pampering since...she had no idea when. Never in her life had she experienced a spa day, so when Weezer had told her that she was going to the salon and spa, she hadn't expected to get a facial and have her nails done—much less spend four hours there.

However, she had to admit, she might want to do that again in the near future.

She stepped outside and turned toward the coffee shop. Immediately, her gaze locked on Weezer, who sat at a table with two of her children.

Chablis and Merlot.

She only knew it was them based on a family picture she'd seen.

Oy. She wished she were within earshot of that conversation since she suspected she might be the topic.

Her and Malbec's return.

Eliza Jane sucked in a deep breath and brought her fingers to her lips. She didn't want to think about that kiss last night. She wanted to forget it along with every other emotion that Malbec stirred within her heart. She needed to focus on her future, and she had no idea what Chablis and Merlot taking time out of their busy day to speak with their mother meant. It could be that Malbec was keen on coming home. Or, at the very least, helping to manage the winery.

Or that he wanted to sell.

The last of those options was the worst, but she wasn't sure about the first two either. Having Malbec around for the first few years while she learned the ins and outs of The River Winery could only be seen as an impediment to the process. He would only get in her way and make things more difficult.

Not to mention, he was a major distraction that she didn't need.

Or he could be exactly what she needed to make everything go smoothly.

She let out a long sigh. She really wanted a fresh cup of coffee, but she didn't want to deal with having to say hello to Weezer and her kids right now. If it were just Weezer, that would be one thing. However, being introduced to more of her family …she just didn't want to deal with that right now.

"Excuse me," a woman said as she maneuvered around Eliza Jane.

"Oh, sorry."

"No worries." The woman smiled. "You're Eliza Jane, right?"

"How do you know my name?"

"It's a small town. Everyone knows everyone." The woman smiled. "My name's Brooklyn Wilde. I live over on the alpaca farm."

"Oh. You must be Alpacino's owner."

Brooklyn laughed. "He's Weezer's favorite." She held her finger to her lips. "But don't tell her I said that. She wants everyone to believe she's not fond of the animals."

"That's not how she tells the story. She's even told me that if I have something I need to hammer out, Alpacino's my guy."

Brooklyn cocked her head. "Well, that's good to hear. Because all she ever does with me is complain." She leaned in and smiled. "But then again, sometimes that's Weezer's go-to. Deep down, she's got a big heart. And don't let anyone in this town tell you otherwise."

"She does run a little hot and cold, that's for sure."

"She hasn't had an easy life," Brooklyn said. "How are you getting along? I know the people of this town can be a bit standoffish with the newbie."

"I've been so busy with work that I haven't had five minutes to breath, much less take in the sights or meet anyone."

"If you need anything, outside of Alpacino's good listening skills, let me know. I'm happy to help." She waved to a man across the street, who looked as if he'd seen better days. "I best be on my way. It was nice meeting you. I'd love to grab a cup of coffee, or better yet, some wine sometime."

"Sounds awesome. I could use a girlfriend in town."

"You and me both." Brooklyn scurried off.

Eliza Jane took one step to her right and nearly walked right into someone else.

"Well, we meet again," the woman from the coffee shop that Eliza Jane had met the first day said. "How are things going at the winery?"

"Good. Thanks," Eliza Jane said. "How did that wine and cheese platter work for you?"

"It was great." The woman adjusted her big sunglasses that hid her eyes. She wore a leopard-print faux fur coat and leather high-heeled boots. "I was just going to head over there to get some more, but not the merlot this time. Any suggestions?"

"I highly recommend the pinot noir. It's excellent. And if you're looking for a white, the Riesling is to die for."

"I'll keep that in mind, thanks." The woman tugged on her black leather gloves. "So, how does it go working with Malbec? I hear he's back in town."

"Well, he's here, but he's not working at the winery."

"He's always got a hand in the family business and he's got a reputation for being quite difficult in general."

"He's not so bad." Eliza Jane didn't want to bad-mouth any of the River family members to a person she didn't know. She couldn't afford gossip getting back to Weezer. That wouldn't be good. Besides, something about this woman set Eliza Jane on edge.

"He's a real charmer, that's for sure. But I'd watch

your back when it comes to him. As well as his brother, Merlot."

"If you know them so well, you must know the winery. Why did you need a recommendation?"

"Just making idle conversation." The woman smiled.

"I didn't get your name," Eliza Jane said as the woman took two steps toward the street.

She waved over her shoulder. "See you around."

"That is one weird person," Eliza Jane mumbled.

"Oh, Eliza Jane. You left your Kindle behind." The girl who checked her out at the spa came running out onto the sidewalk.

"Thanks." Eliza Jane took the device. "I'm right in the middle of an amazing book and I would have been so frustrated tonight when I settled in to read."

"I'm glad I caught you then," the girl said as she let out a big puff of air. "I can't believe *he's* back in town and that Brooklyn is letting him stay with her considering what he's done."

"Who is he?"

"His name is Caleb Ransom. He was accused of killing her uncle." The girl shivered. "Caleb's known for being a troublemaker. I wouldn't be surprised if he did it. Others think otherwise, but there's a reason he stayed away for so long. If I were you, I'd keep my distance."

"If *I* were *you*, I'd stop gossiping about things you

know nothing about." Weezer appeared out of nowhere.

Eliza Jane gasped.

"I didn't mean to scare you, dear," Weezer said. "I was having coffee with my kids and I saw you and wanted to introduce you."

"That would be nice." Eliza Jane couldn't be rude to her boss, even though she really just wanted to get back to work. She wanted to finish with the little cards she'd been working on around the gift shop. She found that having pieces of history that explained the products pushed customers who were on the fence to buy. "Thanks again for bringing me my Kindle."

"No worries. Hope to see you soon." The girl from the spa turned and headed back into the salon.

Weezer looped her hand through Eliza Jane's arm. "Don't listen to a word that young girl said about Caleb. While he's gotten in a bar brawl a time or two, he wouldn't hurt a fly. Unless they really deserved it."

"He looks like he might have been in one of those fights recently."

"If he was, he certainly didn't throw the first punch, and I can guarantee you that it's more about people trying to run him out of town again. Poor kid. He hasn't been given a fair shake in this town. I'm hoping Brooklyn can help turn that around. Of course, she has her own set of issues that she needs to work through. But they are both good people."

"That girl certainly didn't think so."

"Well, that girl is a gossip."

Eliza Jane chuckled. "My grandfather would be telling me to close my trap right about now, but you do know that's what the entire town says about you, right?"

"Of course, they do. But I could care less." She smiled. "I bet you got an earful about me in there."

Eliza Jane arched a brow. "It was mostly all good."

"I doubt that. This town likes to tell crazy stories about me, and only about half are true." Weezer tugged her across the street. "What was your favorite tall tale about me today? And be honest. I really want to hear this."

Eliza Jane swallowed. "But that would be gossiping, and I know how you feel about that."

"Oh, good Lord. I really like you," Weezer said. "And I love what Jenna did with your hair. I'm so glad she didn't cut much off. And those highlights... They are to die for. Malbec's eyes are just going to pop out of his head." Weezer stopped in front of an outdoor table. "Kids. I'd like you to meet Eliza Jane." She waved her hand, not giving Eliza Jane a chance to comment, which was probably a good thing. "This is Chablis, my eldest daughter, who happens to be a firefighter in the next town over. And this fine gentleman is Merlot. He's a parole officer for the county," Weezer said with a beaming smile. Her chest puffed out with pride. "They also help out during harvest and other busy times at the winery."

Eliza had never been told that information before. According to Weezer, other than the three youngest, none of the kids had a hand in the business.

"It's nice to meet you," Eliza Jane said, doing her best to keep her emotions at bay. Just because the family was active, didn't mean she would be pushed out, but she'd feel a lot better when everything was in writing. Once that happened, she could breathe.

"We've heard a lot about you." Merlot stretched out his arm. He looked a lot like his brother and father with his broad shoulders, dark hair, and blue eyes. But he had his mother's scrutinizing stare.

As did Chablis.

She also had her mother's perfect complexion.

"I hear you're staying in the cottage," Chablis said.

"I am. It's very comfortable. I really like it there." Eliza Jane sat in the chair that Merlot offered.

She shifted uncomfortably, feeling as though he was looking her up and down—and not in a good way. It was more like he was sizing her up for lunch.

"I invited Eliza Jane to our family gathering this weekend," Weezer said as she stuffed her hands into her oversized jeans' pockets. She had a nice figure, but her clothes were always two or three sizes too big. "But I'm still glad you are both getting a chance to meet her now. We can be an overwhelming bunch to get to know all at once."

"That's an understatement." Merlot fiddled with the small wooden coffee stirrer.

Chablis glared at her brother. It was hard to miss the venomous stare, but Eliza Jane tried to ignore the nasty vibe that circled the table.

Hopefully, it had nothing to do with her, but she doubted it.

"I hope you're settling in well at the winery," Chablis said.

"Oh. I am. It's a lot to process and take in, but I'm learning and figuring things out." Eliza Jane crossed her legs and did her best to appear relaxed, even though she was a ball of knots inside.

"She's really smart and has some great ideas," Weezer said. "I'm excited to implement some of them."

"Since when do you take ideas from other people?" Merlot snapped his gaze toward his mother.

"Merlot," Chablis said in a hushed voice. "This is not the time or place."

He nodded.

"My brother speaks very highly of your skills in the winery and out in the vineyards, as do my mom and dad," Chablis said. "It takes a lot for my mother to give a compliment."

"That's true," Weezer said. "I've always believed that praise is like candy. Only to be handed out on special occasions and when deserved."

Eliza Jane had no idea how to take that analogy, but she decided to roll with it. "I'm enjoying working at

The River Winery and am looking forward to learning so much more under your folks."

"And Malbec." Merlot arched a brow. "I heard he was there all morning barking out orders." He shook his head. "Which was a total shocker, considering all he wanted to do a week ago was sell the place. Now, his mind is flipping about like a fish out of water."

"That's not true." Weezer folded her arms.

"Yes, it is." Merlot cocked his head. "But we shouldn't be having this conversation right now."

Eliza Jane squared her shoulders. She really didn't want them to hold back on her account. Honestly, she wanted to know what they thought about her and Malbec, and something told her that Merlot spoke his mind no matter the company.

Kind of like his mother.

"Malbec is helping Eliza Jane out this week and mulling over a few things," Weezer chimed in.

"There is nothing to consider." Merlot pulled the top off his paper coffee mug and peered inside as if it would refill itself.

"Stop acting like a child." Weezer reached for Merlot's ear.

He jerked but was unsuccessful in avoiding the grab. He let out a long breath. "Mother. Really?"

"I need to go. Perhaps the two of you can buy Eliza Jane a sandwich." Weezer dropped her hand to her side.

"I really should get—"

Weezer interrupted Eliza Jane. "Nonsense. You need to eat. Take a half hour or so and get to know these two. I'll see you at the winery shortly. You, me, and Malbec can go over some things then."

Eliza Jane opened her mouth but quickly snapped it shut. Besides, she'd learned not to argue too hard with Weezer. She might as well take this opportunity to get to know Merlot and Chablis, do a little digging into the family history, and figure out the family dynamics before the big dinner in a couple of days. It might also give her some insight into how she should proceed with any future business dealings, contracts, and even simple conversations.

"All right." She let out a long breath. "I could use a light lunch."

"Good. I'll see you in an hour." Weezer turned on her heel and marched off down the street with her head held high and her combat boots smacking the pavement as if she were being sent off into battle.

"You have no idea what you've gotten yourself into," Merlot said under his breath.

Eliza Jane had no expectations regarding any of the older siblings because she hadn't heard much about them. The younger ones had a bigger hand in the business, and people she'd worked with had worked with the twins and Zinfandel.

But no one had had any dealings with Merlot, Chablis, or even Riesling.

At least, not that Eliza Jane knew about.

"Actually, I do." Eliza Jane wouldn't let a moody man get under her skin. Especially when she already had Malbec to deal with. "But I have a couple of questions for you."

"Before we grab some sandwiches?" Merlot asked with a hint of sarcasm.

"Merlot," Chablis said under her breath. "Stop being such an asshole. Your problem has nothing to do with Eliza Jane."

"I'd like to know what your problems are with me." Eliza Jane tilted her head and smiled. "You don't even know me, yet you're very hostile toward me."

"It's not you." Chablis flattened her hand on the table. "It's our mom and her unwillingness to sell the winery—which some of us believe would be the best all-around."

"Is that what you believe?" Eliza Jane asked.

"The answer to that question depends." Chablis didn't blink.

"On?" Eliza Jane held her breath.

"Whether or not Malbec is willing to give up Napa Valley and come home. And if Merlot and I are willing to help out more than we already are."

Eliza Jane narrowed her eyes. "Not to sound too selfish, but where does that leave me?" It was starting to sound like she was fucked no matter what the Rivers did with the winery.

"That's a very good question," Merlot said. "If we all come back, why do we need you?"

"Why the fuck do you need to be so goddamned mean?" Chablis tossed a napkin at her brother. "There is no need to come in so hot. Mom put her in the middle of this. It's not her fault."

"*Her* is sitting right here." Eliza Jane waved her hand. "And do you even want to work at The River Winery?"

"I would love to work with my brother." For the first time, Merlot's mouth cracked a smile, and his eyes lit up as if he'd just seen the most beautiful sunrise known to man. "That is if he wants to come back. But if this is a part-time thing, then I want to sell. I'm tired of the bullshit. So, to answer your question, yes, I want the winery. But if, and only if, my family is all there. And to be totally frank, that means you can take a hike."

"Well, at least I know where I stand in your eyes." Eliza Jane rubbed her hands on her jeans. "Does the rest of the family feel the same way?" She got the impression that the twins and Zinfandel might have different opinions. Even Carter seemed to enjoy having Eliza Jane around, but she couldn't be sure.

"This is a complicated family, and so much is up in the air that most of us are unsure of *what* to think of you," Chablis said. "I know my parents seem to really respect you, and I personally don't see the need to send you packing. I think Merlot is speaking out of emotional frustration with our family. There are some things you don't know about. That even *we* don't understand when it comes to my mom and—"

"The secret." Eliza Jane closed her eyes for a brief second. Malbec was going to kill her, but this was her future she was fighting for. She wasn't about to lay down and let someone take it away.

Chablis gasped.

Merlot's jaw gaped. He cleared his throat. "Excuse me?"

"I know some dark secret drove Malbec away, and that's why he refused to come home and run the winery."

"Are you and my brother screwing?" Chablis asked. "Because the whole town seems to think you are, and he wouldn't tell anyone that unless he was drunk or in bed with them."

"Just because Faith, the tarot card reader, had some weird vision and told Mom doesn't mean it's true," Merlot said. "Besides our brother wouldn't ever become involved with anyone working at the winery again."

Again?

That was something Eliza Jane would have to discover later.

"No. I'm not sleeping with Malbec," Eliza Jane said with an annoyed tone. She rubbed her temple. "But I don't want your family selling the winery to some big corporation. That wouldn't be good for me. And, frankly, it would be a horrible decision for your family heritage."

"At least you're honest about that," Merlot said.

"I try to be as truthful as I can about most things," she admitted. "It's best for me if your family doesn't sell, but it's also best if I get to run it with Malbec having a minimal hand in it while he's still working in Napa Valley."

Merlot frowned. "That's not what we want. It's only putting off the inevitable. If Malbec doesn't come back in a permanent role now, we'll just have to sell this place later when our folks are too old to really take care of it."

"My brother is right. We feel like we're in a now-or-never situation," Chablis said. "This isn't personal. It's business. And we know our younger siblings see what they believe is the best of both worlds, but we're worried about the toll this is taking on our folks. They aren't getting any younger."

"Have you talked to Malbec? I mean, really had a sit-down with him about all of this?" Eliza Jane swallowed the thick lump in her throat. Battling one River was one thing.

Battling the entire clan? That was something entirely different.

"Not in detail, but we plan on it," Merlot said. "He's either coming home, or we're selling. There is no in-between. It's just that simple."

No. It wasn't. But Eliza Jane wouldn't argue the point just yet.

She would get that contract and then force Weezer's hand before the family gathering.

If not, she was leaving Candlewood Falls.

For good.

10

———

MALBEC

Malbec finished ringing up a local customer who'd purchased a wine-tasting package for their bridal party. It seemed the news of a new wine-maker had made it around the neighboring towns, and people were coming to check it out and buy more wine.

While it was a bruise to Malbec's ego, he had to admit, he was happy about the traffic coming into the building.

And even more so with the new personal touches that Eliza Jane had added to the gift shop and the wine-tasting room. It was the little details that made the difference. The place cards with their fun facts or the ribbons around the boxsets of wine that they hadn't done in the past.

It amazed him that she'd only been there a few days, and yet, she'd managed to make enough simple changes to make the space feel more like home.

The bell over the door rang as his mother breezed through with a big smile plastered on her face. "Good afternoon." She held up a big bag. "Your father made his famous fried chicken, and I happened to slave over some mac and cheese last night, which I reheated before I left. Are you hungry?"

"I'm starving." His stomach growled. "Tammy, mind looking after the store while we go up to the office?"

"Not at all, Mr. River." Tammy, one of the girls that had been working at the winery for a good decade, said.

Malbec followed his mother up the old wooden stairs. As a kid, he used to love sitting at his mother's feet, chomping on some fresh grapes as he watched her work. He'd learned so much from coming to the winery with her as a small boy. He remembered having to beg and plead to be allowed to spend any of his free time there, even giving up going to activities with his siblings or other friends just so he could learn more about how to make the best wine in the world.

He cherished those memories.

Once inside the unchanged office, he found the card table and unfolded it while his mother took out a tablecloth.

Another tradition when he entered high school and worked the summers side by side with his mom.

His father would bring over homemade lunch, along with the rest of the kids, and they'd have a family picnic. It wasn't every day, but it was often. Malbec missed those moments. It was something he wanted if he were to ever have a family of his own.

However, at thirty-eight, he wasn't getting any younger. And the older he got, the pickier he became. A vision of Eliza Jane jumped into his mind. Actually, she'd always been there—from the moment he'd laid eyes on her. And no matter how hard he tried, he couldn't shake the attraction.

It wasn't the physical part that concerned him because he knew that would fade. He'd been attracted to beautiful women before who wanted nothing to do with him. Rejection was all part of the dating game.

It was her intellect and her humanity that made him want to know her on a deep, emotional level. And that was terrifying. He had no idea he had that many levels.

"Here. Let me help, Mom." He took the big plastic container and opened it. The smell of his father's breading seeped out into his nostrils and made his mouth water. "I've died and gone to heaven."

His mother laughed. "This is why I married your dad."

"Then why did you divorce him?" Malbec paused and stared at his mom. That was not a question anyone ever said out loud. "I'm sorry. That was rude."

"No. It's a legit inquiry, and no one has dared to ask in a long time." She took her seat, waved a napkin, and placed it in her lap before folding her hands and resting her elbows on the table. "It was in part because of the secret."

"The one that you were supposed to tell me when I was ready to take over the winery?"

She nodded.

"Are you going to tell me now?"

She shook her head.

"Why not?" He joined his mother at the table, opening the mac and cheese and plopping a heaving spoonful onto his plate. It was warm and gooey, just the way he liked it, and it gave him something to enjoy and savor instead of dealing with the frustration of his family's legacy.

"Because it would destroy the man you are, and I won't be responsible for doing what my grandfather did to my father, and what they both did to my husband and me—and, indirectly, my kids. It has torn us apart enough, and I've decided to let that damn dirty little secret stay buried with them."

Malbec wanted to be able to let it go. He should. However, it had been a thorn in his side for so long, he wasn't sure it was possible. "It was so important to Grandpa that it always be protected. And he believed the only way to do that was to have the main owner have the knowledge and power." He waved a piece of fried chicken. "I struggle to understand what that means. And the fact that it's been a wedge between us for over a decade, it's going to be hard for me to just drop it. I mean, I told you just a year ago that, under no circumstances would I ever consider running The River Winery until you told me."

"I know," his mother said. "And that's my fault because I'm the one who made it a big deal."

"So did Grandpa."

She laughed. "He could be so freaking dramatic when he wanted to be. And let's not forget, I was barely an adult when my father turned this place over to me. Your dad was in law school, and I was still a scared kid. Your grandpa had a lot of pull and used that secret to control me. I didn't want to do that to you, and I sure as shit wasn't going to let that old coot do it either."

"Is that why you almost never let us be alone with Grandpa?" Malbec always thought it weird that if his grandfather wanted to take him on a fishing trip or something, his father would take time off work and go with them. Malbec rarely spent any time alone with his grandfather. And whenever he did, his mother would take her father aside and wave a finger under his nose. And when he got home, she always grilled Malbec on what kinds of conversations he and his grandpa had, to the point where Malbec didn't even want to go anywhere with his grandfather anymore. And not just because of the way his mom was, but because his grandpa would get weird, as well.

"That wasn't until you were about fourteen, and my dad wanted to tell you the truth."

Malbec coughed. "Why, when I was so young?"

"To control your actions. And I never wanted to do that."

He laughed. "You do realize that's funny coming from you, right?"

"I'm not as manipulative as you think I am, and my reasons were always to protect you, not to force you to do what I wanted—which is what my father did. I believe those are two different things."

"Maybe so, but you pushed me away because of it."

"I did." At least she was admitting it now.

"Why?" If she wasn't going to tell him the secret, he needed a really good explanation. Better than half the excuses she'd given over the years, which weren't much of anything. Most of the time, she'd tell him that it was none of his business. Or that he didn't need to know to run the winery. Or that when she'd leave him a note to read when she was dead and gone.

That one had been his favorite, because knowing Weezer, she would leave him a note telling him that he was better off not knowing.

That would be the ultimate screw-over.

"I thought I was protecting you from the kind of pain I have in my heart. I'm still doing that. And as a mother, I'll never stop." She dropped a piece of half-eaten chicken to her plate and wiped her fingers on her napkin. "Honestly, what haunted my father and grand-father doesn't matter. The only thing that does is what we do moving forward. I'm taking that secret to the grave and letting it die with me."

His mother could talk in circles for hours, and he

didn't have the time. He planned to meet Chablis, Riesling, and Merlot for drinks at five, and then Eliza Jane for dinner. He glanced at his watch. He was shocked that Eliza Jane wasn't at the winery already. He knew she'd had a big day at the spa, on his mom, but that was hours ago.

"Is this stupid secret going to be a deal-breaker?" His mother took her chicken bone and tossed it into the trash along with her paper plate.

He followed suit. "I haven't agreed to anything." Oh, shit. This wouldn't go over well. He'd have to downplay it. "However, I *am* considering having a bigger presence and potentially coming back full-time at some point."

His mother jumped to her feet. "Oh. Malbec. That makes me so happy."

"I haven't made up my mind, and I do need you to do something for me." He stood, holding his mother by the forearms.

"Anything, if it means you're coming home."

Far from it. "Taubet Liquors wants a meeting."

"No. No. A big fat no. How does that equate to you and Eliza Jane running this place together?"

He arched a brow. His mother hadn't taken into account Merlot and Chablis, who, based on their texts this morning, would be around a lot more if Malbec moved home.

That said, they were also pushing to sell, especially Merlot. He could use the money. He was tired of dealing with the long hours during harvest and the family drama. And Malbec didn't blame him.

"It doesn't, but like I said, I haven't made a decision one way or the other, and I think you should at least hear what they have to say. You can always say you're not interested."

"I'm saying it now." His mother packed up the extra food and tossed it into the bag with more force than necessary. "Why waste their time and mine?"

"Because they will be here on Monday."

His mother glared. "That's in four days. You'd better cancel it before it's too late."

"I already confirmed it this morning."

"Talk about underhanded," his mother mumbled.

"Like mother, like son."

"I have half a mind to take you over my knee." She plopped herself back into the office chair. "I brought you into this world. Don't think I won't take you out of it."

"You love me too much to do that."

"Don't press your luck, kid." She pulled open one of the drawers. "I wasn't going to do this until Monday, but since you just gave me a really big pill to swallow, turnabout is fair play." She shoved an envelope under his nose.

He leaned against the desk. "What's this?"

"Eliza Jane's employment contract."

"Why does she need one at this juncture?" He pinched the medal tabs, easing out the papers inside. It wasn't a very thick contract, and the first thing Malbec noticed was that his father had drawn up the papers. "I thought she was going to be an employee, not a contract-worker for the time being."

"Part of this is for the line of wines she wants to create with her name and any new wine she might develop with our label."

"I'm aware of that." He scanned the words on the page. It all seemed standard until he got to the part where his mother had offered a percentage of not only profits but also ownership. Granted, Eliza Jane had mentioned that, but he hadn't expected his mother to so easily give up a piece of the pie.

And that could potentially happen before he or his siblings ever owned a stake in the family business.

Quickly, he flipped to the next section where he read a passage stating that when he and his brothers and sisters took full ownership, the provision for Eliza Jane could not be undone. She would be named in the will. He read it two more times.

Malbec tossed the paper across the office. "No fucking way. You can't do this. You've lost your fucking mind."

"That's no way to speak to your mother."

"I don't give a shit." He raked a hand across his head and turned to face his mom. "What the hell do you think you're doing?"

"Exactly what that contract states."

"Why the fuck are you doing it? She's not family.

She means nothing to any of us, and you've made your damn point. I'm here. I'm listening. I'm even considering moving home." He paced in front of the large oak desk in the center of the office. He ran a hand across his jaw and shook his head. It wasn't like she'd done this to spite him for having Taubet Liquors show up in town. She'd just found that out, and that contract had been created at least a day ago.

"If you don't calm down and stop swearing, I won't continue with the conversation."

He closed his eyes and counted to five before blinking. "Why are you giving her a percentage?"

"You don't think it's fair to give her a piece of her label."

He planted his hands on his hips. "I'm fine with her having a stake in her label. It's the stake in the vineyard that I'm struggling with."

"Too bad. What's done is done."

"Is she holding something over your head? Does she know the secret? Is she blackmailing you with something? Because I can't imagine you doing this out of the kindness of your heart. It makes no sense."

"She's not holding anything over my head. This was my idea. And it doesn't have to make sense to you."

"I can't believe Dad drew those up and didn't say a damn word to me." Oh, but he could. His dad disagreed with Weezer, but he didn't often go against her. That was either because he knew the cards wouldn't play out as she expected.

Or he knew something the rest of the family didn't.

This didn't feel like either and it left a bad taste in Malbec's mouth.

"It wasn't your business." Weezer swiveled back and forth in the big leather chair with her arms folded across her chest. "I didn't plan on telling you until after I had the chance to go over the contract with Eliza Jane and we both signed it, though."

"Jesus, Mom. You'd do that? To me? Or all of us kids?"

"I'm not doing anything to you," his mother said. "That girl hasn't a single family member left in this world—"

"So, you decided it's *our* responsibility to adopt her or some weird shit."

"This doesn't change anything."

"Are you crazy? It changes everything. And not just for me, but for all of my siblings. Do they know what you've done?"

"No," she said flatly. "And you're not going to say anything to them until that contract is signed. If you do, there will be hell to pay."

"You should have waited until after Eliza Jane put her John Hancock on it, because now that I know you've literally lost your marbles, I'm going to do everything in my power to make sure you can't give away what rightfully belongs to my siblings and me."

His mother jumped to her feet. "It's not rightfully yours. I don't have to leave you a penny if I don't want to. What your generation fails to understand is that inheritance isn't a right. It's a privilege. And if I choose to leave this to Brooklyn Wilde or the church down the street, no one could stop me." She poked herself in the chest. "This is my winery. Not yours. Not your father's. And not your siblings'. It's mine. And I'll do with it what I see fit. If you have a problem with that, don't let the door hit you on the way out." She pushed past him, pausing at the door and glancing over her shoulder. "Oh, wait. You've already done that, and you got kicked in the ass." She disappeared down the stairs.

"Fuck," he muttered. "Well, I guess I don't have to redeem myself after all, because Eliza Jane isn't going to like me after I tell her to get the hell out of my cottage."

Eliza Jane

Eliza Jane paused at the main gate to the winery and stared at her cell.

Malbec: *Meet me at the cottage. I need to speak with you. It's urgent. I'm there now. I'll wait.*

Well, crap. That couldn't be good.

She suspected that Merlot or Chablis or both had gotten ahold of Malbec in the last half hour and said something that bothered him a great deal.

Eliza Jane: Can it wait? I have work to do.

What she really needed was to find out if Weezer had the contract, and if it was ready to sign. Once that was out of the way, it didn't matter what any of the River kids had to say.

Bile smacked the back of her throat. She didn't like feeling as though she were an underhanded bitch. Maybe if her father were still alive, she wouldn't feel the need to put down roots in one place.

Especially this place.

Memories bombarded her brain.

"You'd love The River Winery," her father said. "It's got rolling hills and beautiful sunrises. They are like nothing you've ever seen. And the grapes are crisp and full of flavor."

"But you've never tasted the wine." She sat on the floor with her legs crossed as her father rocked back and forth in his big recliner. He always enjoyed telling her about his travels, especially when it included visiting wineries and vineyards.

"Oh, but I have. It was a long time ago when the vintage was much better."

"Is the wine no longer good?"

Her father shook his head. "I'm sure it's fine. The grapes are superb." He leaned forward. "But someone like you could do it much better. You have your great-grandfather's gift." Her father sighed. "Your grandfather never had the passion, and while I've always wanted to be really great at winemaking, I just don't possess the talent."

"You make a really nice bottle," she said.

"You're so kind, my lovely child."

She always enjoyed it when her father called her his child, even as an adult. It reminded her of when she used to go apple or strawberry picking with him and they'd make jam or pie. In those moments, she never once missed her mom.

He'd been her everything, and she missed him so much. Her biggest regret in life was not understanding all the little nuances between her father and her grandfather. Their relationship was different. They obviously loved each other and had a halfway decent working relationship.

But they also had demons. Ones she couldn't comprehend. Maybe if she had, she'd understand now why she'd felt compelled to come to New Jersey and make it her home the moment Weezer sought her out.

Malbec: No. This is work-related.

She glanced up to see Tammy waving good-bye to a couple of customers.

Eliza Jane: I'll be over shortly.

"Hey, Tammy." She scurried toward the main entrance.

"Oh. Hi. Eliza Jane. I was told you might not be back today."

"By whom?"

"Both Weezer and Malbec." Tammy stuffed her hands into her overalls' pockets. That was her signature style, and the look was quite becoming on the woman. "Weezer mentioned you were in town with Merlot and Chablis, and Malbec said you had meetings."

"I do have to discuss some things with Malbec." Though what, she had no idea. "Anything of interest happen here today?"

"Not really. Although we've had a lot of foot traffic —more than usual. And our cash register receipts are up, so that's good."

"Would you say more than last year?"

"Oh, yes." Tammy nodded vigorously. "People have asked about potential changes and who the new wine-maker is. It's all good stuff."

"Next week, I'll make sure I'm more available."

"I've given out your card and sold a few of those tours you added. I'd say business is already looking up."

"Well, that's a step in the right direction." And now it was time to make sure that continued. She waved her cell. "I'll have this with me if anything needs my attention."

"I'll be sure to call if I can't handle anything, but don't worry. I've been doing this for a long time. You're in good hands."

"Thanks. If I don't make it back this afternoon, I'll be in before the sun rises." She tucked her phone into her purse and tossed it over her shoulder. It would take her ten minutes to walk the path if she did so at a swift pace. She opted for a slightly slower one, taking as much time as she could to clear her mind. She needed to prepare herself for whatever argument she was walking into. She might not know Malbec well, but one thing she'd learned was that he wore his emotions on his sleeve.

Even in text messages.

He wasn't a happy camper.

The cottage appeared through the trees. It was a quaint log-style structure. Small, but it did the trick, and she could see herself living there for a year or two. She didn't need much, and it was close to work and away from people. While she could absolutely handle any customers, the rest of the world left something to be desired.

Especially right now.

Malbec sat on the front stoop, playing with a blade of grass. He glanced up. As soon as they made eye contact, he slowly rose to his feet. "Thanks for meeting me."

"You really didn't give me much choice."

"Can we go inside and maybe have a glass of wine and sit down?"

"It's only four in the afternoon."

"It's five o'clock somewhere. And I know after the day I've had and the conversation we need to have, I could use an entire bottle." He held her gaze for a long moment.

"I'm not sure drinking will make whatever you need to get off your chest better."

"I've spent the last hour contemplating whether or not to go into the cottage and toss your things out the window or tell you to take a hike and watch you pack your stuff and leave."

Her need to know why would likely get her the kind of answers she didn't want to hear. But the truth was always better than a sugar-coated lie.

Or a secret buried with the dead.

"Now why on Earth would you do that?" she asked.

"Can we please go inside and have some wine? I'll do my best to talk calmly and rationally about business." His chest rose as he took in a deep breath. "I want to hear your side, and I will keep my emotions in check while you speak."

"You're not making any sense, but I'm happy to listen to whatever it is you need to say." She pulled out her keys and unlocked the door, then swallowed. The idea that he had a set of keys and could have come in and gone through her things sent fire through her veins. She had personal and private belongings that her father had given her when he died. Like that picture of her great-grandfather with the sign that read *The River's Edge Winery*. The longer she stayed at The River Winery, the more it looked and felt as if it had been take in this very spot.

She needed to go to the library and check out the book that Jenna had told her about. Hopefully, that would give her some answers about the winery and put to rest this weird feeling she had about that stupid picture.

"What kind of wine would you like?"

"Either a pinot noir or a cab would be nice. But, honestly, I'll take whatever you've got."

She set her purse and keys on the table by the front door and strolled past the couch to the small kitchen. She yanked open the fridge and found some cheese. She set it on a platter, along with some high-end crackers before finding a bottle of pinot. She set the tray on the coffee table and poured two very generous glasses, handing him one before kicking off her shoes and flopping onto the sofa, tucking her feet under her butt. She took a large chunk of cheese and set it meticulously on a cracker and placed it on her tongue. Closing her eyes, she let her tastebuds go to town.

He sat on the other end, practically on the armrest as if he had to be as far away from her as possible. He stared at the television, which was in the opposite direction as she was, while he held his glass and masterfully swirled his wine.

She waited for a long moment for him to talk, but he said nothing, just sat there in silence.

"So, what's so important that you have me playing hooky for the rest of the day?" She brought the glass to her lips and took a long, slow sip. The red liquid flowed easily down her throat. It wasn't the best year, but it still had a rich, robust flavor, and it didn't burn.

That was half the battle.

"I need total honesty. Can you give me that?" he asked without turning his head.

"That's all I've ever done."

"I'm not sure I believe you."

"That's your problem, not mine." She leaned forward, taking a few more crackers and some cheese. Stuffing her face before she drank half the bottle was a moral imperative. The last thing she needed was to get hammered in the middle of the afternoon in front of Malbec River.

Especially when he was in a mood.

Which was most of the time.

"Did you ever meet my mom before she came knocking at your door asking you if you wanted a job here?"

"No." Eliza Jane didn't like the way this conversation had started. She took another large gulp of wine. "Why?" She always had to know the why.

"I'm getting there."

She let out a long breath. "I take it this is going to be much like the Spanish Inquisition."

"A little bit." He took a long, slow drink. "How many other wineries did you try to create your label with?"

"None." She held up her hand. "But I was offered two contracts. I turned them down."

"Why? What was the problem?"

"The first one was a really shitty deal. I would get five percent of sales, but only after I paid back the cost of making the wine."

"So they were essentially offering you a loan and a place to make your label." He finally turned his head, catching her gaze.

"Sort of. I would never have ownership of the label, and that was a deal-breaker. Plus, they didn't have a vineyard. It was just a winery, and they often changed where they purchased their grapes. I came in to save their reputation. I did that, and I left."

"I see. And the second one?"

"My father was dying, and it wasn't the right time." Tears burned her eyes. She blinked. No way would she cry in front of Malbec. Not right now, anyway.

"That's fair." He shifted, turning completely in her direction. He lifted both his legs and sat cross-legged. "I wish I remembered your father and grandfather's visit."

"It was about twenty years ago."

"I would have been eighteen. I guess it's possible I could have already gone off to college, though I didn't go very far."

"You went to Cornell University."

"You did your homework." He smiled. It was a kind smile. One that invited people to get to know him. And yet, he didn't do it very often, at least that she could tell. "Where did you go?"

"University of California."

"That's a solid education," he said.

"Why do I get the feeling you're beating around the bush and avoiding what you really want to discuss?"

"Because I am," he admitted. He snagged a few crackers and pieces of cheese and chewed slowly, staring at the ceiling. "I like you. And for the few days I've known you, I've enjoyed working with you and getting to know you better. But I'm not happy with the way things seem to be playing out."

"What things?" Her heart hammered in her chest. She didn't have to be a rocket scientist to figure out what this conversation was likely leading up to, but she wasn't about to bring up the topic of the contract and the deal his mother had offered—not until the contract was signed. Weezer had said they'd meet in the morning.

That meant that Malbec would have to deal with being put off for a night.

"Who came up with the terms of your employment contract?"

She coughed and gagged. Setting the glass on the table and pounded her chest. "You need to speak with your mom about that."

"I already did. Now I'm talking to you, and I want some honest answers." He scooted closer.

"What did your mother say?"

"We're not playing that game," Malbec said. "All you need to know is that I saw the contract."

"Then there is nothing to discuss. You know the deal. All that is left to do is for me to sign it."

"Oh, no. That's not happening." He shook his head. "Though what I don't understand is why the hell my mom would give you a percentage of my family's winery." He pressed his finger over her lips when she opened her mouth. "I have no problem with what she offered when it comes to your label. Hell, I might be inclined to be more generous over time if the label proves to be financially worth it. But to take ownership away from my siblings? From my niece? That's fucking nuts. Please make me understand why she'd do that. Are you some long-lost relative and I should be ashamed for mentally undressing you and kissing you?"

She pushed his hand away and covered her mouth as she stifled a laugh. She shouldn't find any of that statement funny, but she did. "No," she said. "We are not related, though I'd rather you not picture me without my clothes on. That's really creepy."

"I find you insanely attractive, and I'm drawn to you, which is why this is so damn hard. I'm frustrated and angry, but I'm sitting here, next to you, and I want to forget all the reasons I'm so mad at you and take you into my arms and do more than imagine what you look like without fabric covering your skin."

"It's best if you stay on your side of the sofa."

He chuckled, but it was cut short. He set his glass on the table. "Who came up with the terms of the contract?"

"We both did," she admitted. She wanted to lie to him or avoid the truth, but his vulnerability struck a chord in her heart. It shouldn't, but it did. Besides, she was as drawn to him as he said he was to her.

She suspected that was a recipe for disaster.

"Did you ask for it, or did my mom offer?"

That was honestly a loaded question. Because when Weezer had come to her offering her a job, part ownership hadn't even been on Eliza Jane's radar. Weezer had put that thought into her head. It had been a passing comment in one of their many video meetings, but it was Eliza Jane who'd come up with the numbers, though only after they'd hashed out the label agreement.

However, that was after Weezer had promised that her children weren't interested and were on board with Eliza Jane having a piece of the pie.

Which had clearly been a bit of a lie.

"I'm going to be more honest with you than I'd planned."

"You thought about lying to me?" He arched a brow.

"Not exactly." She tucked her hair behind her ears. "I wanted to put you off. But I have some unanswered questions of my own, and maybe you can help me."

He scooted even closer. For a second, she thought she should feel uncomfortable, but in reality, she felt like she was sitting with a close friend she was having a slight disagreement with.

But this was more than a little tiff. This was huge. And her heart tightened a bit over how she'd been so willing to cheat him out of what had been in his family for generations. She had no right to be so selfish. The River Winery hadn't belonged to her family, and she had no right to ask for a stake in it.

Not even when it had been offered.

Of course, when she and Weezer had first discussed the possibility of a more permanent role in The River Winery, it was a year or two away. Eliza Jane would have had some time to get to know the town of Candlewood Falls as well as everything about the winery and the River family. She would have been able to ease herself into a decision.

But that'd all changed the second Weezer manipulated her family.

One the one hand, Eliza Jane couldn't blame Weezer. However, Malbec wasn't the kind of man who responded well to being backed into a corner. That was why she was willing to be so honest. He deserved the truth. At least, the parts she could tell.

And she needed to understand why she felt so connected to something that wasn't hers or even a part of her past. She'd worked at a dozen wineries, and none of them had seeped into her bloodstream like this one had.

"The original plan had been for me to work for a year and see where things were. But I don't think that was ever your mother's plan."

Malbec reached for his wine and downed half the glass. "And what do you think she was up to when she hired you?"

"Exactly what you're thinking."

"And how do you know what that is?"

"It's the only possible scenario, given what's transpired," she said.

He took her hand and laced his fingers with hers, rubbing his thumb over her skin. "All I got from her was that you were alone in this world and that she wanted to give you an opportunity. That your father made an impression, and when she heard he'd died, she felt compelled to offer you a job. It's not the first time my mom has taken someone in like that. She also mentioned that she could do whatever she wanted." He let her hand go. "But I don't get this matchmaker thing when it comes to giving you part of the winery. If she wanted us together, why promise you something that you'd get if we were to be—to be—a thing?"

"Wow. That was really painful for you to say, wasn't it?"

He laughed. "No. The only thing causing me distress right now is trying to understand my mother's motives and why my dad is going along with it. I mean, he drew up the contract, and it shocked me that he was so willing to give up that much of the business."

"I can't believe you saw the contract and I haven't."

"You really haven't gone over it yet?"

She shook her head. "I was supposed to sign it this afternoon, but between meeting Chablis and Merlot and now this, well...it's been pushed off until tomorrow."

"Fuck." Malbec reached into his back pocket and

pulled out his cell. "I better let them know I'm not meeting them tonight."

She reached out and folded her hands over his. "Please, don't cancel on your siblings because of this. I don't want to be the cause of any family fights. Today was hard enough."

"Why? What happened with my brother and sister? Did they say something that upset you? Insult you? Because I'll take care of them."

"Oh. My God. Do you hear yourself? You're giving me whiplash."

"You usually do that to me." He pinched the bridge of his nose. "But, honestly, I don't have the brain power to deal with Chablis and Merlot tonight, considering what's happened. I'll see them first thing in the morning. Do they know about the deal you struck with my mom?"

"No. But they either want you to talk her into selling, or they want you home so they can come work with you. And that kind of implies there is no room for me in either situation. Merlot was the most vocal on his thoughts on that." Well, crud. That was way too honest. But Merlot was a bit of a jerk, so she shouldn't feel bad for tossing him under the bus.

"How so?" Malbec asked.

"He made it clear that I wasn't welcome."

"He actually said that?" Malbec rolled his neck. "Did Chablis agree?"

"Merlot didn't see how I could add value, and

Chablis only said that this wasn't personal but business," Eliza Jane said. "The thing is, I got the impression they are more inclined to sell than to have you home. Is that true?"

"No. But there is a different issue," Malbec said. "I wasn't honest with you about Merlot and why he switched gears and became a parole officer."

"What do you mean?" She searched her brain for the conversation that she and Malbec had had about his brother, Merlot. It hadn't been that long ago, but she'd learned so much about the family in such a short time that some of it had jumbled together. "He went to Cornell, as well, right?"

Malbec nodded. "Chablis finished the same degree that I did before the firefighter academy, but Merlot only spent two years at Cornell before transferring to Potsdam and switching to criminal justice. That switch in degrees came on the heels of my big fight with my mom, which was also right after I broke up with my longtime girlfriend."

"Someone who worked at the winery?"

He cocked his head. "How do you know about that?"

"I'm learning that everyone knows everything in small towns."

He laughed. "Well, Racheal, my ex-girlfriend, was a local. She started working in the winery when we were in high school and stayed on through college. She had a lot of high expectations, including being in charge of some things, and that wasn't going to happen when Merlot came on board. That bothered Racheal and caused some problems between us. I didn't know that my little brother had a crush on her."

"Oh. That's never good."

"Nope. And he felt the need to be the one to tell me that she was cheating on me."

"That had to hurt."

"It did. However, I didn't want to believe it at first. But when a friend of ours was wrongfully accused of murder, she believed that he did it. Between that and me finally seeing the truth about her, well, it put an end to our relationship, and Merlot had a new interest in criminal justice."

"That sucks for your friend."

"It did," Malbec admitted. "But the bigger reason he switched gears is that he felt I betrayed him when I left for Napa Valley, and he wanted nothing to do with the wine business to spite me. He's still angry with me, which is probably why he was a shit to you today. If he thinks I want to keep you on, it will remind him of Racheal, and that was always a sore subject with him for a lot of reasons. I never would have put her in a higher position as an employee, but if she and I had worked out, well…" He shrugged.

"Merlot wasn't a total shit. But he did seem a bit all over the place."

"He is, and it gets even more complicated," Malbec said. "I don't know if he'd prefer we sell and be done with it all, or if he hopes we'll reconcile our differences. I mean, we get along great, but there is this undertone that doesn't go away. And the world thinks we hate each other because he acts like he hates me in front of people."

"That would be a true statement." She leaned in, wanting to feel the warmth from Malbec's skin. "However, it's obvious that Merlot admires and respects you. He wants to work with you. He'd rather the winery stay in the family."

"You're just saying that because it serves you."

"It does serve me, but the contract isn't signed, and my fate is so far out in the balance, I feel off-kilter." His lips were a milliliter from hers, and that made her dizzy. "I want to be here. I deserve to have some skin in the game for my talents and my efforts. You'd want the same in my shoes."

His mouth came down on hers hard, and his tongue slipped between her lips. There was no mistaking his intent.

And there wasn't a chance in hell she would stop him.

11

———

MALBEC

Malbec pulled her as close to his chest as he could. His tongue found hers and curled around it in a dance that felt familiar. He couldn't explain why he was so compelled to hold her, but he didn't want to let her go.

Of course, he waited for her to push him away since his kiss came out of nowhere. Besides being totally inappropriate, if this went any further, it would complicate things to the point of no return.

She wrapped her arms around his shoulders and straddled him. Her passion filled his veins with a fire he hadn't felt in years.

Actually, he'd never had a woman touch his soul this deeply.

It wasn't just about how his body reacted to her touch. It was about how his heart filled with passion, and his mind desired to know everything about her.

His pulse kicked into high gear. He struggled to fill his lungs with air. He slipped his hands under her shirt and splayed his fingers across her warm skin.

She moaned as he fumbled with the clasp on her bra. It took him a good two minutes before he was finally able to undo the damn undergarment. He almost had to break off the kiss so he could see what he was doing, and he feared if he had to do that, she'd realize her mistake and tell him to stop.

He jerked his head back.

She gasped, licking her lips and staring into his gaze. "What?" She leaned back a little. Her fingers toyed with the hem of her shirt. "Is there a problem?" She lifted it over her head and tossed it across the room. Her bra straps fell off her shoulders.

He tugged at them, exposing her perfectly round breasts and puckered nipples. He groaned. "No," he whispered.

"Then why did you stop kissing me?"

He palmed her cheek. "I don't want you to have any regrets."

"I'm a big girl. You don't need to take responsibility for my actions."

"I'm not," he said. "But I like you, and we will have to work together to figure some things out."

"Yes, we will." She unbuttoned the top three buttons of his shirt and ran her fingers through his chest hair. "And let's not mistake that this doesn't necessarily mean anything. We're just getting it out of our systems."

He arched a brow. "Are you saying this is a one-time thing? Because I don't do one-night stands."

"Good thing it's still in the afternoon then." She pushed to a standing position and toyed with the snap and zipper of her jeans.

He swallowed. Hard. "That's a technicality." Sitting up a little taller, he ripped off his shirt and pushed it aside. "Besides, once is never enough to put down to experience. You have to have a second opportunity to make sure your craving has been satisfied, and you've really put it behind you."

"Are you ever going to shut up and take me to bed?"

He gave her a little shove, and she fell back onto the mattress, which was directly across from the sofa. It took him all over two seconds to rid himself of his slacks and another five to yank hers to her ankles.

She scooted up to the head of the bed, giggling. It was such a sweet sound. It tickled his ears and gave him warm goosebumps. He could listen to her laugh all day long and never get bored.

Her tanned skin glowed in the sunlight beaming through the windows. She had to be the most beautiful woman he'd ever laid eyes on. Never in a million years had he believed that he could feel this much in such a short time, but Eliza Jane had brought him to his knees. One time wouldn't be enough to satisfy his tastebuds.

A week wouldn't come close to taming his desire.

He needed months to peel back the complicated layers that made up Eliza Jane. And the process needed to be done right. It couldn't be like ripping off a bandage.

No.

Eliza Jane wasn't the kind of woman who gave herself over easily. He would have to earn that trust.

And he planned to do just that.

He kissed her from head to toe, leaving no part of her untouched. She tasted like a sweet nectarine. He teased her, bringing her to the brink of climax, only to pull back until she begged him not to stop.

She rolled him to his back and climbed on top, rolling her hips and grinding. Her desperation spilled over to him, and he clutched her hips, digging his fingers into her soft skin. He gritted his teeth and swallowed a guttural groan.

"Yes." She arched her back. "Malbec."

"Slow down." He tugged at her hair, pulling her to his chest and taking her mouth in a hot kiss, swirling his tongue around hers much like their bodies thrust against each other.

"I need you." She nibbled on his neck, sucking and kissing wildly. "Please."

He flipped her to her stomach, pulling her to her knees as he stood at the side of the bed. He entered her slowly while reaching around with one hand to find her hard nub. He rubbed gently in a circular motion as he moved inside her, entering her deeply but slowly.

"Oh, my God. Yes." She glanced over her shoulder and pushed harder against him, increasing the pace.

There was no way he would remain in control, no matter what position he tried. She would always take charge.

And he honestly enjoyed that about her in more ways than one.

He leaned forward, holding both her hips, and thrust hard. He continued to do so until she convulsed around him, her climax overtaking him, forcing his to spill out. He continued for a few moments, at a much slower pace, rubbing her back, letting his fingertips feel every curve of her spine as they caught their breath. He collapsed onto the bed next to her, pulling the spare blanket over their bodies and hugging her to his chest.

She kissed his neck and wrapped her arms around his middle, letting out a long sigh.

Running his hand up and down her supple skin, he searched for the right words, but he came up with nothing. He had no idea what to say, so he chose to keep his mouth closed for a change. However, eventually, he'd have to come up with something. They needed to converse, and he needed to sound intelligent. And, of course, he couldn't insult her or make light of what'd just happened.

He blinked.

He swore he'd never get involved with anyone who

worked with him ever again. Hell, he'd kept his so-called relationships out of the wine business altogether. Racheal had made sure that he never wanted to mix any kind of business with pleasure ever again. She'd honestly thought that his family owed her something.

They didn't owe her a damn fucking thing.

But this was different.

God, he hoped it was different.

"You just tensed up like an angry bird." She patted the center of his chest.

"Sorry." He inhaled sharply through his nose and let it out slowly through his mouth.

"Did you just come back to reality?"

"A little bit."

"Yeah. Me, too." She pulled the blanket tightly around her body and sat. She scooted to the foot of the bed and snagged both wine glasses.

He found his underwear and put them on before taking the beverage. He took a long sip. "Oh, that's good."

"Better than sex?"

"Hell, no. I don't think anything can top what we just did. Ever."

"Flattery might give you a second opportunity."

"Good to know." He chuckled. "I've got some other compliments if you care to hear them."

"Let them simmer for a few hours."

He lowered his chin.

"It's just a possibility. I'm not making any promises." She raised her glass. "It's been a very long time, and I was horny."

He tapped his wine against hers. "Here's to being hard-up."

"We're pathetic." She took a sip and then set the drink on the nightstand. "I know I shouldn't bring this up while we're still in bed, but that probably wasn't the smartest move."

"Nope. But you're the one who said we needed to get it out of our systems ." He curled his fingers around the back of her neck. "Are you cured of your desire for me?"

Playfully, she smacked his forearm. "I plead the fifth."

"Well, I'll take the stand and tell the truth."

She reached over and covered his mouth. "That won't be necessary. I get the picture. But you know this can't keep happening. We are oil and water. And whether you like it or not, I'm signing that contract tomorrow."

"I'm sorry. But that contract won't be offered." He slipped from the bed. Sleeping with her had been a mistake. It wasn't because he didn't care for her, though—because goddamnit he did.

More than he wanted to admit.

But he was about to crush her heart flat.

Right now.

"That's not for you to decide," she argued.

"No. But I know my mom, and she'll pull back

because of everything that is going on. She'll draw up one with the label, and I'll ask her to increase the percentage for that. But the ownership of The River Winery is off the table. I'm sorry. No matter what we do, that's my family's business. Whether we sell today or not for decades, it belongs to my siblings and me and any future children any of us might have. It can't go to you or anyone else. I can't allow it."

She jumped from the bed, holding the blanket around her body. "You couldn't say that before you climbed into my bed?"

"I didn't think I had to." He found his pants and hiked them up. "I told you that you could have your line of wine and work at the winery. There is plenty of room for you here. There is no reason for you to go find employment elsewhere. But ownership is out of the question."

"No. You can't do that to me. I won't let you." She reached over to the nightstand and opened the drawer, finding the picture of her great-grandfather. She didn't understand why she thought this might push Malbec to understand why she needed this so badly or why she'd fight for it until the bitter end. "I belong here." She shoved the picture under his nose. "I have a feeling this image was taken here. I planned to go to the library and do some digging, but I haven't had a chance yet."

Malbec took the paper in his hands and glanced between her and the picture. "Who is this?"

"My great-grandfather," she whispered. "It was the

vineyard he owned that he gambled away. My grandfather never forgave him. He lost his wife over his gambling and drinking problems. I didn't know him, but I'm told I have his same passion and talent for winemaking."

Malbec fell back onto the bed and ran his free hand across his head. He couldn't believe what he was staring at. The sign was identical to the one in the history book in the library.

The original name for the winery. The one that had been changed when his great-grandfather went legit.

Or at least that was what he'd been told.

And what the history books said.

But his grandmother had written that book.

"Get dressed," Malbec said.

"Why?"

"I've got something I need to show you, and it has to do with that sign your great-grandfather is holding."

Eliza Jane

Eliza Jane didn't like being in Weezer's house, especially when the woman wasn't home. Even more so when Eliza Jane had only been there once for a breakfast meeting on the back patio, which had a great view of the vineyard. But this felt as though she were invading her boss's privacy.

"You can sit down," Malbec said.

"I'd rather stand."

"If you're worried about my mom coming home, she won't. She's with my dad at his place. Once they sit down to dinner, unless they get into a fight, that's where they remain for the night."

Eliza Jane stared at all the family pictures hanging over the sofa. "How did that work after your parents divorced?"

"The only change was that we had two homes." Malbec sat cross-legged on the floor by the fireplace as he pulled out one photo album after the other, flipping through the pages. "My dad came over here every day when school got out and helped with homework. He drove us to practices or after-school activities and, obviously, they had marital relations because my mother got pregnant twice after they ended their marriage." He tossed another album aside. "But they didn't fight as much, and there was a lightness in the house that hadn't been there before."

"What was the reason they gave for divorcing?"

"They told us it was easier to love each other when they had a little space, but we all knew it had something to do with our grandpa. But only Chablis and I knew that it was all centered around whatever that fucking secret is all about. That was until my granddad decided to let everyone know that he had a dirty little secret. Then it was a mad dash to find out what it was. Unfortunately, he died, and my mom won't tell anyone."

"I never understood why no one knew where my great-grandpa's winery was. I get there was shame over what he did. But it was a very long time ago."

"Older generations are weird." Malbec set a ratty old scrapbook on his lap and opened it. "Here it is. Come, sit with me."

She let out a sigh and joined him on the floor.

"Tell me something," Malbec said. "Do you know anything about the bet your great-grandfather made?"

"Nothing other than he lost everything over it. My grandpa would never talk about it, and my father pretended that he didn't know much. But that was bull-shit. He just didn't want to start trouble."

"What about after your grandfather died? What did your father say then?"

"My grandpa died two months before my dad, and he was sick for a year. So, not much."

Malbec lifted his gaze. "I'm sorry. That's really rough."

"It was," she admitted.

"What about your mom?"

"She ran out on us when I was five. I haven't seen her or talked to her since my tenth birthday."

"Jesus. I thought my family was fucked up, but that's just wrong."

She shrugged. "According to my dad, my mom never

wanted me, but it was too late for her to have an abortion, and my dad always told me that he was madly in love with me from the second my mom showed up six months pregnant."

"That's pretty cool of your father."

"As crazy as he and my granddad were, he was a pretty cool guy. He did his best to make sure I always felt loved and was cared for, especially when my mom left."

"I can't imagine that was easy."

"It wasn't that hard, either. I mean, she made it pretty clear that she didn't like or want my dad or me. I'm not even sure why she married him, except for the fact that maybe she thought he might be able to make some money and spoil her. But that never happened, so she moved on to greener pastures."

"Have you ever tried to find her?"

"Nope, and I don't want to." Eliza Jane had no desire to find a woman who would ultimately reject her —and that she knew for a fact. "The last time I saw her, she told me that when I got some tits, I should come visit and she'd show me how to get a real man."

"Fuck. That's crude."

"That's my mom." She leaned over and stared at the album in his lap. It was filled with vintage photographs. "What are you looking for?"

He flipped a few more pages. "This." He tapped an image of an older man and a woman standing in front of a sign that read: *The River's Edge.*

The exact same sign that was in the picture she had of her great-grandfather. The only difference was that this one had been taken in front of the old cottage and next to it was the new sign that read: *The River Winery*.

"That can't be," she whispered.

"That's what I thought when you showed me that image, but there is no way that's some kind of weird coincidence." He tapped the album. "They are identical."

"How old is that picture?"

"I don't know. It was probably taken a few years before my grandfather was born." Malbec turned his head. "My mother told me that she always felt like she had to protect this dirty little secret in order to make sure the traditions of the family and the winery were intact. I always thought it had something to do with the fact that, for the first decade, this winery was illegal. I wondered if maybe there were still issues with back taxes or something. I had no idea that it could be something like winning it in a bet. Not to mention, no one in this family likes to gamble—especially my grandfather."

"Maybe that's why." She ran her finger over the sign in Malbec's family picture. She couldn't believe that she'd found her great-grandfather's vineyard. "Your mother knew about this. That's why she sought me out." A flash of anger filled her heart. She sprang to her feet and paced in front of the sofa. She planted her hands on her hips and tried not to stare at all the happy smiles in the family images displayed proudly on the walls.

This land started out as her great-grandfather's.

And then he gambled it all away during a drunken night at the poker tables. Which, according to her grandfather, became a way of life until he died.

"This still doesn't feel right." Malbec tugged the picture out of the album and set it on the coffee table before putting everything away. He stood and curled his fingers around her forearms. "Winning a winery over a gambling bet isn't a big enough secret for my mother to push me away. She wouldn't do that. There has to be something more to this story. What else can you tell me?"

She blinked out a tear. "All I know is that my grandfather shamed my great-granddad. He was so embarrassed by his father's drinking and gambling that he almost never went into the winemaking business at all. It wasn't until my father became interested in it that they joined forces."

Malbec pressed his lips over hers for a brief but tender kiss. "I can see how a bet like that could tear your family apart. It would be devastating to lose a business in that manner. But shit like that happened a lot back then. And to be totally frank, I don't see that as a dark enough secret that my grandpa or mom would be willing to lose any of their family members over it."

"I see your point." Eliza Jane had to admit that it made no sense for Weezer not to say how the family came into the winery. "If your great-grandfather won the winery fair and square, there would be no reason to be ashamed or concerned about what anyone thought."

Malbec tilted his head. "That's what concerns me."

"Do you think somehow your great-grandfather cheated or something?"

"I don't know," Malbec said. "But I intend to find out." He pulled her into his arms.

She stared into his deep blue eyes. She wanted to turn and run. She didn't want to care for him or have any real emotions when it came to Malbec. Especially when his family winery could be tied up in her family in such a negative way. "What is going on in your mind right now?" she asked.

"I have a million and one questions, but only my mother and father can answer them. And even then, we might not know the whole truth."

"If your family won this winery fair and square, I'll walk away. But if not, you know I'm not going to sit idly by."

He brushed her hair from her face, running his thumb across her cheek.

Not only did she feel a connection to The River Winery.

She felt one to Malbec.

He made her feel as though all her hopes and dreams could come true, and that no matter what, things would work out.

Even this mess.

"I need you to give me a little time to talk to my folks."

"I want to be there when you do," she said.

"My mom will take that as an act of aggression. Perhaps you should let me—"

"No."

"You still don't trust me," he whispered as his lips pressed against hers. "I don't want to hurt you."

"But you also don't want me to have an ownership stake in this winery."

He jerked his head back. "I brought you here and showed you that picture. I didn't have to do that. I could have kept it a secret from you and done what every other generation ahead of us has done. But I'm not willing to continue with that game. Either you and I are in this together, or we're not. Either way, you're going to have to trust me."

"That's not going to be easy."

He kissed her nose before bending over and snagging the picture. "Let's go back to the cottage, have some dinner, and sleep on it."

"You expect to spend the night at my place?" Her stomach filled with butterflies. She had to admit, she liked the idea of waking up in his arms.

"I don't want to stay here and risk seeing my mom and confronting her before we're ready. And I can't go to my dad's right now, so it's either I stay with you or crash on the sofa in the office at the winery."

"Oh. I feel so manipulated right now."

"I doubt that." He laughed. "But, seriously, it will give us some time to talk about the best way to approach this conversation with my mom and dad. And even before that, maybe we can go look at that history book."

"Yeah. I really wanted to do that."

"I should warn you. My grandmother wrote it."

She rolled her eyes. "That doesn't give it much credibility."

"Except she was notorious for subliminal messages. We might find something hidden in there if we look hard enough." He laced his fingers through hers. "Let's get out of here. I need some wine, and I'm feeling like I need to lie down."

"Oh. My God. Do you really think you're going to get a little more action today?"

"A guy can hope."

MALBEC

Malbec blinked open his eyes and rolled to his side. The sun peeked through the window as it filled the morning sky. He reached for his cell. It was six-forty-five in the morning. He glanced at Eliza Jane, who was still blissfully asleep on the other side of the bed.

Their night had consisted of a bottle of wine, some Chinese takeout, and a lot of lovemaking.

He made no apologies for any of it.

Only he worried about what the future held because he had a bad feeling in the pit of his gut.

He slipped from the bed and made his way to the small kitchen, where he pulled down a mug and put it under the Keurig, hoping it didn't make too much noise. Tapping the screen on his phone, he pulled up his text messages.

There were about half a dozen from Merlot.

They might have a strained relationship, but when push came to shove, they always had each other's backs. But their issues when it came Racheal were deep, and they cut right to the heart. Merlot had never gotten over the fact that Malbec had given Racheal a higher position in the winery when Malbec was the manager. He'd done so because it was Merlot's turn to work the vineyards that summer. It was a rite of passage, but Merlot saw it as Malbec being on a power trip and wanting his girlfriend at his side. No matter what Malbec said, Merlot didn't believe him, and he went about doing whatever he could to make Malbec's life miserable.

And Merlot succeeded the day he snapped a picture of Rachael playing kissy-face with one of the managers over at the apple farm. It was obvious that Merlot had gotten great pleasure out of telling Malbec about Racheal's indiscretion. But three months later, Merlot was in Racheal's bed.

Six months after that, Malbec received a phone call from his sister, Riesling, informing him that Racheal had dumped Merlot for greener pastures. Merlot had a chip on his shoulder the size of Texas ever since.

And he blamed Malbec for what happened with Racheal—which was ridiculous.

Malbec scrolled to the last text, which informed him that Merlot and Zinfandel would be at the cottage by seven to discuss the future of The River Winery.

Fucking wonderful.

He took the five steps to the bed and sat next to Eliza Jane. She had a right to be a part of this conversation.

Merlot would have a shit fit.

He bent over and kissed her cheek. "Good morning, beautiful."

She stretched. "What time is it?"

"Too early, but Merlot and Zinfandel are on their way over. They will be here shortly. I'll make you some coffee and eggs, if you'd like."

"What? Why the fuck are they coming over?" Frantically, she brushed her hair from her face and scooted to a sitting position.

"They want to talk about my plans for the future," he admitted. "Which I have no idea how to answer, especially since we found that picture." He rolled his neck. The few times they'd brought up the subject last night, the conversation got heated, so they'd decided it was best to leave it until the light of day. They knew they needed to address it, but not until they knew more.

But the question was how and when they should bring in his family. That part they didn't see eye to eye on.

"You need to tell them. And we need to confront your parents," she said. "And why not start right now?"

He really didn't want to argue first thing in the morning, but he was left with no choice thanks to his brother and sister. "You need to let me manage this with my family. Please trust that I'm not trying to screw you out of anything. I'm trying to uncover the truth about that picture."

"I think we know the truth. And your mother knows that my family started this winery, and that's why she's giving me a piece of it."

He pinched the bridge of his nose. They'd had this same exact discussion last night. "And your great-grandfather lost it to mine in a poker game."

"Until we know your family's secret, we don't know the whole story. Because the whole illegal sale of liquor story doesn't really fly."

"They were probably embarrassed by the way my great-grandfather—"

"Don't go making assumptions," Eliza Jane said. "If you don't start asking the tough questions, I will. How much time do we have before they get here?"

"About ten minutes." He palmed her cheek. "I know you want to jump in with both feet. But I know my family. We have to play our cards right, but we don't have the right hand yet. We need to find out some information first, and the best place to start is at the library and then with my father. From there, depending on what we find out, we can have discussions with my family. But Merlot isn't the person to start with. Not when you and I are sleeping together.

"Why?"

"It's a very long story."

"Give me the CliffsNotes version."

He let out a long breath. "We were once in love with the same girl. Only I had no idea about the feelings he had for her until I'd already been with her. And even worse, when she and I broke up, she went straight to Merlot."

"Did they get together?"

He nodded.

"That's kind of gross," she mumbled.

"And it shows she loved this winery more than she loved either of us."

"How long were you with her?" Eliza Jane asked.

"I spent four years with her, and Merlot only six months. All she wanted was to become Mrs. River. She didn't care which one of us she got. She only wanted to be a part of the winery."

"I'm probably going to hate myself for asking, but why was that so important to her?"

"It was a status thing. She grew up dirt-poor on the outskirts of town. She thought if she was with someone who had a solid family business, someone who had a little bit of money and could give her respect in the community, it would get her what she wanted."

"Where is she now?"

"She ended up marrying a politician and is our local congressman's wife."

"That's a tough life. I think I'd feel like I was constantly on display."

"That's exactly what she wanted. Only she just recently had an affair, and the news posted a picture of her with some guy. They can't identify him since his face is covered, but she's not denying it."

"That's a shitty thing to do." She twisted her body to the side and set her feet on the floor. "I'll just get some coffee. It will only take me—"

Knock. Knock.

"Shit. They're here." He jumped to his feet and did a little dance, looking for his jeans. He hiked them up while she scrambled to find her clothes. "You'd better hurry. Merlot isn't a very patient man, and everyone in this family has a key."

"That really sucks. I think I'm going to change the lock." She pulled a shirt over her head. "I can't do this without coffee. Why the hell did they come over so early?"

"I suspect it's because they have jobs and have to be at work by eight or nine. Or maybe they know something we don't."

"I guess that makes sense." She hopped on one foot and nearly fell over as she pulled up a pair of shorts. "Put some cream and sugar in my coffee while I use the bathroom. And toss a pillow and blanket on the sofa so it looks like you slept th—"

"They aren't going to believe that for one second." He yanked her to his chest and gave her a big, wet kiss. "Zinfandel already believes you and I should be together and all but bet me—"

"She what? I'm not sure I want to hear this."

"You probably don't." Malbec laughed. "And,

Merlot, well, he'll take one look at the situation and read it correctly."

"This isn't making me feel any better." She raced across the room and opened the bathroom door. "I might not come out."

"You'd better. Or this love machine might not come out and play tonight."

"Oh, my God. Don't ever say that again. It's not sexy at all, and it won't get you laid."

"Yeah. My baby sister was right. I've got no game at all."

Her laughter continued to echo in the room even after she'd closed the door.

Time to find out what had his brother and baby sister showing up at nearly the crack of dawn.

He pulled open the door and plastered a smile on his face. "Good morning," he said, doing his best to keep his frustration to a minimum. No reason to make his siblings his adversaries in all of this. It was hard enough dealing with Eliza Jane.

"Not really," Merlot said.

"Ignore him. He's been in a bad mood ever since Racheal—"

"Shut up." Merlot glared.

"What about Racheal?" Malbec might have ended it because she'd cheated, but when he looked back on the relationship, he could see how all she cared about was what others thought about her, and that drove him nuts, especially when she complained about his mother. Racheal would talk about all the changes she'd make to the winery when his mother was no longer in charge. And those things wouldn't be good for business, but he let her voice her opinion because Racheal just needed to feel important, and he'd thought he loved her.

So, when Malbec found out that she'd set her sights on Merlot, he lost his shit and told Merlot all about Racheal and her plans.

That conversation hadn't gone over well, and it had driven a deeper wedge between his brother and him. Even after Racheal broke Merlot's heart, Malbec couldn't mend the relationship with his brother—which he so desperately wanted to do.

"She had the fucking nerve—"

"I told you to be quiet," Merlot interrupted Zinfandel. "It's none of your business." He sat down on the chair next to the sofa and leaned forward, resting his chin in the palm of his hand. "It doesn't matter anyway. I told her to fuck off."

"She's got you all in knots. Again." Zinfandel tossed her purse to the floor and made her way to the chair where she placed her hand on Merlot's shoulder and squeezed. "You should tell Malbec. He's not going to judge you, and it's going to come out eventually anyway."

"It has nothing to do with the winery."

"Oh. But it will," Zinfandel said. "It's going to be front-page news."

Merlot groaned as he lowered his head. "I fucked up good."

"What do you mean by that?" Malbec glanced over his shoulder as he heard the bathroom door creak open.

The last thing he needed right now was for them to clam up, and that's exactly what they'd do in front of Eliza Jane.

"I can't talk about it in mixed company," Merlot said. "And again, right now, it has nothing to do with the family business."

"If you're worried about Eliza Jane, she's in the shower. And she takes fucking forever. She uses all the hot water. It's kind of annoying."

The sound of water rattling through the pipes filled the room.

"We've got a good twenty minutes." Malbec maneuvered around the chair and sat down on the sofa. He reached out and placed his hand over his brother's knee. "I'm here for you. No matter what. I've got your back."

Merlot tilted his head. "This is bad. Like Mom is going to yank off both my ears bad."

Zinfandel handed Malbec her cell.

He stared at a picture of Racheal in a compromising position with a man. He'd seen the image before, but he hadn't paid much attention to it. Bringing the phone closer, he expanded the screen, making the image larger. "What am I looking at?"

"That's me," Merlot said. "Racheal showed up at my apartment about a year and a half ago with bruises on her arms and stomach. She said her husband was hitting her."

"Jesus. That's horrible."

Merlot inhaled and let it out with a big sigh. "I don't believe it was true. I think she used that to try and get me into bed."

"Did it work?" Malbec asked. "Did you sleep with her?"

"No. Actually, I didn't," Merlot said. "But as you can see, that picture is a little damning and suggests we might have. The worst part is that there are more pictures of us together."

"What kind of photographs?" Malbec asked.

"Me holding her hand. Me comforting her. They are all innocent, but they could be taken out of context."

"She still wants to ruin us," Zinfandel said. "That's why she set up for that picture to happen. She's the one who sent it to the press."

"She's going to release the rest of the images," Merlot said.

"Doesn't she know this will destroy her and her husband?" Malbec ran a hand over his mouth and chin. The winery didn't need this kind of press right now. It didn't matter that Merlot wasn't a full-time employee. He was a River and Weezer's son.

Not to mention, he was a parole officer, and it would likely hurt his career.

"She hates her husband, so I don't think she cares about that." Merlot leaned back and folded his arms across his chest. "Mom is going to kill me. She hates Racheal."

"That she does." Malbec glanced at the ceiling. "But you didn't do anything wrong."

"Maybe not. But we don't know how she's going to spin this," Merlot said, venom dripping from every syllable. "She could make me out to be some kind of predator." He shook his head. "I can't believe I let her manipulate me again."

"Don't blame yourself." Malbec saw no point in being mad at his little brother. What was done, was done. Now, it was time to figure out how they could make this go away so it didn't hurt the business. But more importantly, so it didn't affect his brother.

"Has she hinted how she's going to play this out? Or exactly what she wants from Merlot?" Malbec asked.

"Nope," Zinfandel said. "And we've tried to get her to talk to us, but all she has to say is that payback is a bitch."

"Payback for what?" Malbec muttered. She'd used that phrase numerous times over the years, but he wasn't sure exactly what he'd done—other than ending the relationship—that would cause such hatred. Especially this many years later.

"When you broke up with her, she'd been telling everyone that you had bought her a ring and were just waiting for the right time to propose," Merlot said. "She was utterly humiliated and felt betrayed by you."

"So why not come after me directly? Why is she using you this way?" Malbec asked. The blood flowing through his veins came to a boil. He didn't need to deal with this and the issues with how his family came to own The River Winery. If those two things came out at the same time, it would bring down his family business for sure, and then there would be nothing for him to sell.

Or come home to.

"She got over it."

"I've learned that woman doesn't get over anything. She holds grudges. And she's got a big one against me, too." Merlot rubbed his temples. "No one knows this but Zinfandel, Riesling, and whoever Racheal told."

"And I only know because I had to kick his ass the other day to get it out of him." Zinfandel plopped herself on the edge of the bed and then sprang right back to her feet. "You and Eliza Jane had sex on that bed this morning, didn't you?"

"I wish," he said with a laugh. "The two of you kind of ruined those plans."

She sat on the coffee table. "I guess you've got more game than I gave you credit for."

"Can we focus on something other than Malbec's sex life?" Merlot asked.

"Sorry," Zinfandel said. "Go ahead."

"After Racheal and I broke up, she said she was

pregnant with my kid. Shortly after that, she said she miscarried, and I didn't bother to show up at the hospital because I didn't believe her."

"I wouldn't have either."

"She sent me the paperwork a week later with the proof," Merlot said. "I had Riesling check to make sure it was real. Racheal was pregnant and she did lose the baby. But we don't know if it was mine, but I plan on finding out."

"My money is on the fact that it was someone else's," Zinfandel said. "Nothing that woman does is real. Besides, if it was yours, she would have been screaming it from the rooftops because that would have given her a piece of our winery. And that's exactly what she wanted."

Malbec waggled his finger. "That's a really good point. I bet she knew it was someone who didn't have money, power, or respect, and that didn't serve her purposes."

"How the hell did both of you fall in love with someone so heartless and cold?" Zinfandel asked.

"That is a very good question," Malbec said. "But I think I can speak for both of us when I say that we know how to spot a snake when we see one."

"I wish I could be so confident," Merlot said. "My taste in women sucks."

Malbec leaned forward and squeezed his brother's knee. "You'll find someone. And she won't be a Racheal. I'm sure of it."

"Speaking of that." Merlot tilted his head. "I'm not trying to be a total dick here, but Eliza Jane is getting too entangled in our family business."

"We'll get to that in a minute." Malbec needed to have that discussion, but he wasn't quite done with the Racheal topic. "Zinfandel, don't you have a reporter friend who works on Capitol Hill?"

"I do. And I've called Adrian. But that will only give us about five minutes before the story goes viral. We won't have enough time to counteract it."

Malbec rubbed the back of his neck. "We need to find out sooner than later what she's up to, and I think I know how to do that." Shit. This could backfire in a thousand different ways, but it could also be the most brilliant plan he'd ever had.

"How? Because there is no way in hell Racheal will talk to you," Merlot said.

"No. But we have a secret weapon." Malbec smiled.

"And what's that?" Zinfandel asked.

"Eliza Jane," Malbec said with a little too much pride.

"How so?" Zinfandel asked. "What can she do for us?"

"Corner Racheal and find out what the fuck she's up to." Malbec raised the phone. "She can help change the narrative because she has what Racheal has always wanted, and no one that she's met after Merlot or me has really given her that."

Malbec stood and strolled to the nightstand. He pulled out the two pictures.

"And what does Racheal really want?"

"The respect of the people in Candlewood Falls. Her husband isn't well liked as a congressman. As a matter of fact, he's going to be voted out of office next term."

"That's probably true," Zinfandel said. "She's always wanted to be the queen of Candlewood Falls."

"In high school, when she didn't win homecoming queen, she went ballistic," Malbec said. "I'd never seen anyone so angry. I seriously thought about breaking up with her then, but she seemed to get over it."

"Rumor had it she was the one who destroyed Gigi's dress," Merlot said. "And knowing what I know now, I wouldn't put it past Racheal."

"Neither would I," Malbec said. "But if she thinks she has an ally in Eliza Jane, she might spill the beans."

"Why would she think that?" Merlot asked.

"We have two problems we have to deal with, and I have a feeling they might collide pretty quickly." He handed the images to Merlot. "That's Eliza Jane's great-grandfather. According to her, he lost *The River's Edge Winery* in a poker game."

"Jesus. That's the exact same sign." Merlot blinked as his gaze diverted back and forth.

Zinfandel stood behind him, and her jaw slackened. "That's impossible. We've always owned this land. Our great-grandfather bought it from some guy named Elijah James, who was moving his family out west."

Malbec sat on the corner of the bed. "What if the big secret that has been tearing this family apart for generations is that we didn't obtain this winery fairly?"

"Losing a bet is fair," Merlot said. "I wouldn't do it, but lots of people do. Especially back then."

"I agree. And if that's how we ended up with the winery? It's nothing to be ashamed about. But I've had a few heart-to-hearts with <om, and based on what she said—or hasn't said—about this damned secret, there is something fishy about how we came into ownership."

"Are you saying our great-grandfather might have cheated or something?" Merlot asked.

"I don't know," Malbec said. "But don't you think it's time we found out once and for all?"

"If it means we can put this dark cloud that has kept you from coming home and the rest of us at arm's length behind us, then hell yes," Merlot said.

"All right, then. Time to bring Eliza Jane into the conversation and get this ball rolling." Malbec took both his sibling's hands. "If what I suspect is true, Eliza Jane deserves to have a piece of the winery. And just so you know, Mom was writing that into her contract."

"Jesus," Merlot whispered. "Then it must be true. She'd never give up a percentage to anyone. Hell, she was going to make Ashling's dad sign a prenup if he ever married Riesling."

"That's because he's an asshole and a deadbeat," Malbec said. "But she wouldn't bring that up to anyone she approved of, or loved and welcomed as part of this family. She wants all of us to be happy and find our soul mates. Just like she did with Dad."

"Oh, shit," Zinfandel said. "He's got it bad."

"I can tell." Merlot finally put a smile on his face. "I have to admit, she is hot, and I do like her personality—even if I give her a hard time. And I think she's good for Malbec."

"I agree."

"Oh. My. God. Just shut the fuck up," Malbec said. "I need to take a shower, and we need to go to the library and then have a powwow with Mom and Dad." He waved his finger. "While I'm in the bathroom, you'd better not say anything weird or embarrassing to Eliza Jane. Got it?"

"Who? Us?" Zinfandel raised her hands. "Never."

"Wonderful," Malbec muttered as he padded toward the bathroom. It was going to be a weird and long day.

13

ELIZA JANE

Eliza Jane reluctantly took Malbec's hand when he laced his fingers through hers as they strolled from the parking lot toward the library. "We're really giving this town something to talk about."

"If what I suspect is true, this town isn't going to be talking about the day Mom ran down the street in her housecoat, combat boots, and curlers anymore."

"You left out the loaded shotgun."

"It wasn't loaded," he glanced in her direction with a big, goofy smile. "For the record."

"I don't know, I've heard stories at the salon."

"Did you hear the one about when she chased a boy that dared try to climb into Chablis' bedroom. It didn't matter that Chablis had invited him and that nothing really happened."

"What did your father do? Was he there?"

"Oh. He was, and he laughed his ass off the entire

time as he handed my mom the unloaded weapon. He thought it would be more terrifying if *the* Weezer chased the boy through town than if he did it. And he was right." Malbec opened the door, and the warm air hit her skin.

She hadn't realized that the temperature had dropped outside until the heat inside coated her body. "What happened to the kid? Was Chablis mad?"

"Oh, she was pissed. She wouldn't speak to my mom for a whole week and stayed at my dad's. But she and that boy didn't last much longer. Thing is, if you can't take my family the way we are, you're not going to last. It's probably why we're all still single." He leaned over and kissed her cheek. "You seem to fit in really well."

"Don't go getting any ideas. Just because we're holding hands, and I'm letting you stay at my cottage, doesn't make us a couple."

"Did you just invite me to spend the night again?"

"Since your siblings stole my morning orgasm, yes," she whispered in his ear. "But you better make it worth my while, or I'll just revert back to my vibrator."

"I'm so much better than hard plastic."

"I might have to agree." She followed him through the main part of the library and into the local history section. There were only about ten people in the library, outside of the person sitting behind the desk. And of those patrons, most were parents with their kids getting ready for story time. Her cheeks flushed.

Having kids hadn't been something she'd thought too much about. It wasn't that she didn't want them—because she did—but she'd never stayed with a man long enough to feel as though marriage and a family were in the cards.

And then in the last few years, she had been taking care of her grandfather and then her father and just didn't have time for men or any room for thoughts of a future outside of finding the right path for her career.

Once she figured that out, maybe she could settle down, find a man, and have a few little rugrats.

"The book should be right over here."

"What makes you think we'll find any insight into the situation in a book written by a woman who might have known the truth and wanted to cover it up?"

"We're looking for clues. And I also want to check out some of the other history books from that time." He bent over and pushed a few hardcovers to the side. "Huh. It doesn't look like it's here." He went to the next shelf and continued browsing the titles. "I still can't find it."

"How many copies are in the library?"

"Just the one that I know of." He glanced around. "And I've never known it not to be here." He pressed a hand to her lower back and guided her back toward the front of the building.

The woman at the desk glanced up from her computer screen. "Oh, Malbec. How are you?"

"Hi, Tina. Long time, no see," he said. "How's Greg? The kids?"

"Everyone is great." She leaned back and patted her very round belly. "We're expecting number five in two months. I told Greg this is absolutely the last one. And you want to know what he said?"

"Not until you give him a goalie?" Malbec laughed. "There are five skaters. He needs that sixth person."

"You're not allowed to see him if you're going to encourage him like that." She tucked her hair behind her ears. "You must be Eliza Jane. I've heard a lot about you. I hope you're enjoying our lovely little town."

"I love it here," Eliza Jane admitted. "It's such a quaint place. And working at the winery is a dream come true."

"Even with Weezer being your boss?" Tina asked with a lightness in her tone that indicated she was teasing. For a town that acted as if Weezer were some kind of force to be reckoned with, they all seemed to really like and respect her.

"She's half the fun of the job."

Tina laughed. "So, what can I do for the two of you?"

"I'm looking for that history book written by my grandmother. Malbec kept his arm wrapped around Eliza Jane's waist.

"Oh. I'm sorry. It was checked out the other day." Tina's smile turned to a frown. She brought her fingernail to her lips. "By Racheal."

"My ex-girlfriend, Racheal?"

Tina nodded.

"Shit," Malbec mumbled. "When is it due to be returned?"

Tina tapped at the keyboard. "Next Tuesday."

"Did you see her?" Malbec asked.

"I did," Tina said.

"Did she say anything? Do you know how long she was in town?" Malbec asked. "What about where she's staying? This is such a small town, I'm surprised people weren't talking about the congressman's wife being in Candlewood Falls, especially with the news of her infidelity."

Tina's eyes went wide. "I didn't think anything of it, and her parents live here so I just thought she was visiting them. Plus, I didn't want to bring the press to their doorstep. They have been through so much, what with her dad having cancer and all that."

"It's okay. I understand," Malbec said. "Thanks for your help." He guided Eliza Jane back out into the cool fall air.

She welcomed the slight chill and shivered, staring at the array of colors dangling from the trees. She wasn't quite prepared for autumn, and though she loved every second of it, this current situation put a damper on her mood. "Do you think she could know something?" Her heart lurched to the back of her throat. For selfish reasons, she wanted this little piece of heaven to be where her great-grandfather had created his very first wine. She knew that wouldn't necessarily be a good thing for the River family, but she didn't want to steal the winery from them. If their great-grandfather had won it fair and square, then all she wanted was her equal share.

The question became what did that look like? Was it half? A quarter? Did they split it equally among the River kids and her?

All those thoughts gave her a headache because whatever was brewing between her and Malbec would take a big hit and not in a good way.

"I don't know how that would be possible. I mean, my family guarded that secret with their lives. My siblings didn't know anything about it for years."

"Why is that?"

"I was the only one who was supposed to know because I was meant to take over the winery. It would then be up to me to tell my siblings as they came on, *if* I thought it was necessary."

"And you just thought it was about tax evasion?"

He shrugged. "Something else has been bugging me, and I can't shake it."

"What's that?"

"What on Earth would my great-grandfather bet that was of equal value to the winery?"

Eliza Jane opened her mouth but snapped it shut. That was a good question, and one she hadn't ever thought about or asked. "Did he have money?"

"According to my mother, he wasn't poor since he

was able to buy the land, but we now know that wasn't true. And, as you know, our so-called family heirloom is a fake, but he didn't know that. Actually, no one did until my grandma had it appraised."

"Yeah. That story cracks me—holy shit." She grabbed him by the biceps. "At first glance, you'd think that crest was real, not some cheap knockoff. What if that's what your great-grandfather used to bet."

"But why would anyone take that bet?"

"Because my great-grandfather was a greedy bastard. If he thought it was worth money, he'd go for it. He thought he was that good of a card player. But get a few drinks in him, and he thought he was a gambling God."

"The stories my grandfather told didn't paint my great-grandpa as the kind of man who would do something like that."

"Of course, not. Why would he? Your family had to protect the secret."

"We still don't know exactly what that secret is."

"There's Merlot with your mom and dad." Eliza Jane pointed across the street. "Looks like we're about to find out."

Malbec

Malbec sat at the table in front of the coffee shop and stared out into the street. He really wanted to talk with his mother alone, but she insisted that Eliza Jane be part of the dialogue.

That told Malbec that his suspicions were true.

His mother stepped from the building with his father, carrying two large cups. She set one down in front of him while his father pulled out the chair, helping his mom into the seat. "Eliza Jane is waiting for some food with Merlot."

"Where did you send Zinfandel off to?"

"She's checking in with her reporter friend and trying to get a location on where Racheal might be and find out what she's really up to," his mother said. "That little bitch is a piece of work."

"Wow. You've calmed down a lot in the last hour," his father said with a dash of sarcasm.

"Like you don't agree with me on all counts, including trying to shield our youngest children from this shitshow."

His father lowered his chin. "That's going to be impossible, but you're right. Zinfandel doesn't need to hear this right now. And as far as Racheal goes… She is about to stir up some bullshit trouble, but that's just it. What she's trying with Merlot will blow over because it's not true. And we'll be able to prove it. All of it. Even the shit in the past." His father opened the top of his paper mug and poured in some cream and sugar.

Malbec followed suit. Even though he'd already had

two cups, he could use more caffeine, and he needed something to concentrate on. Part of him felt as if everything going down between Merlot and Racheal was his fault. Had he been a better brother and not had a stick so far up his ass, maybe Merlot wouldn't have gotten suckered by the likes of Racheal.

"I hope you're right," his mother said.

"Trust me. I'm going to take care of Racheal and what she's doing to Merlot. If she's not careful or crosses a line, I'll slap a lawsuit on her so fast it will make her head spin."

"I'd love to make her pay for some of the crap she's put us through." His mom let out a long sigh. "But why would she take out that book your grandmother wrote? It doesn't make sense. How could she know anything?"

"She knows there was a secret," Malbec admitted.

His father dropped his hands to his lap and glared.

His mom gasped.

"Oh. for fuck's sake. I dated her for four years. We lived together in the cottage for two summers. I thought I loved her. Hell, at one point, I thought I was going to marry her."

"At least your taste in women has gotten a whole lot better," his father mumbled.

"What does she know about our dirty little secret?" his mother asked.

Malbec laughed. "Nothing because I know nothing. Jesus, Mom. Eliza Jane knows more than Racheal does."

"Do you tell every woman you sleep with that we have a secret?" His mom cocked her head.

"No," he said with a fair amount of defiance.

"So, you admit you're sleeping with Eliza Jane." His mother folded her arms across her chest and smiled like a proud mother bear. "I knew the two of you were perfect for each other. I'm always right about these things."

Malbec closed his eyes for a long moment and shook his head. He'd walked right into that one. Not that his parents hadn't already suspected, considering they didn't know where he'd spent the night.

"Did you tell her before you slept with her or after?" his father asked with a stupid grin.

"I'm not answering that," Malbec muttered. He lifted his gaze, meeting his mother's head-on.

"You like her. A lot. I can tell." His mother had always been able to read his emotions. And from the get-go, she'd told him that Racheal would break his heart. And every girlfriend he'd brought home after that, she'd made sure that he knew they weren't the one.

He'd always thought she just believed that no one was good enough for her boy.

But she didn't believe that with Eliza Jane. Nope. His mother thought Eliza Jane was his one and only.

He wasn't ready to believe that, but he was certainly willing to find out.

He cracked a smile. It was impossible not to.

"That's not even the point, and you're giving me whiplash with this conversation."

His father slapped his leg. "All we want is for you to be happy."

"And you want me back in Candlewood Falls," Malbec said with his heart stuck in his throat. He had to admit, the concept didn't suck. But only if that meant Eliza Jane would also be here, settling into his hometown and making great wine with him in what appeared to be both their families' winery.

Merlot and Eliza Jane stepped outside. Merlot carried a plate full of breakfast pastries, while Eliza Jane handled a couple of mugs of coffee.

"Sorry that took so long," she said.

"Your timing couldn't be more perfect." Malbec stood, pulling back the chair next to him. He rested his arm on the back and let his hand fall to her shoulder. He squeezed gently.

An awkward silence descended over the group.

Malbec knew this wouldn't be easy for his mother, especially in front of a non-family member, but she was the one who'd insisted that Eliza Jane be present, and Malbec had to agree because this *did* affect her future. "Well, I think we need to address the elephant in the room."

"We're outside," his mother said.

He chose to ignore the comment. "It's time to tell all of us what Grandfather told you. No more avoidance. No lies. We deserve to know what the secret is."

Tears filled his mother's eyes. It was rare that she ever showed that kind of emotion, especially so quickly.

His father scooted closer. "Sweetheart. It's time."

"I know." She nodded. "You must know that your father just found out part of this the other day."

"I don't think that matters," his father said.

"I don't want our children mad at you for something that I hid from all of you."

"We're not going to be mad," Merlot said. "I think we're all just tired of whatever great-grandpa did that made you push all of us away."

His mother nodded. "Eliza Jane. I want you to know that I don't know all the particulars, and I didn't know about your family's involvement until I already owned the winery."

"Okay." Eliza Jane squeezed Malbec's thigh. Hard.

He massaged her neck, hoping to erase the growing tension in her muscles.

"Why don't you backtrack and then show Eliza Jane what was left to you," his father said.

His mother wiped the tears that had fallen down her face. "I was told that my grandfather won the winery during a poker game. That alone is no big deal. Right?" His mother picked at an apple fritter. "My grandfather and father informed me that Elijah James Blue owed a ton of back taxes and that he was gambling to try to come up with the money to pay for it, but he was losing—and badly. My grandfather had been looking for land for months, and he had his sights set on Candlewood Falls, but all of the best pieces of property were already taken. When he saw Elijah James losing his shirt, he took advantage."

"So, he did win the winery in a poker game," Malbec said with some relief.

"That's what I thought." His mother held up her finger. "But he did so using our fake heirloom. That is the first secret."

"Mom. That's not the worst thing in the world," Merlot said. "I'm sorry." He glanced in Eliza Jane's direction. "I realize it's not really cool to bet with something of lesser value, but that doesn't make my great-grandfather a total snake."

"You're right. It doesn't," his father said. "Because if he'd lost, it wouldn't have cost him anything. But it cost Elijah James his entire life. And that burden was too much for your mother to handle. It was a struggle for her at the age of fourteen when she first found out. And it was hard on our marriage. But that's not even the shit kicker in all of this."

"What is?" Eliza Jane asked.

"Sometime after Riesling was born, I learned that my grandfather, my children's great-grandfather, not only took advantage of your great-grandfather, but that Titus William River cheated during that poker game. I don't know how. But my grandfather left me a confusing note, and that is the secret I didn't want to burden my children with and is why I so desperately wanted you to come here and make your wine. It's also why I wanted you to have a small piece of the pie." His mother smiled. "Or, better yet, fall in love with my son —which it seems might still be something in the making."

"Mother. Stop." Malbec let out a long breath. He glanced at Eliza Jane. "Are you okay?" he whispered.

"I don't know," she admitted. "That is a lot to take in. On the one hand, this all could have been mine."

"Yes. It could have," his mother said.

"I don't mean to be rude, but your great-grandfather was willing to gamble it all away," Merlot added.

"I'm well aware of that, too." Eliza Jane blinked a few times. "We always believed he lost it. Not that it was stolen."

"I wish I knew how my grandfather cheated. But I don't," Malbec's mother said. "I also wish I'd tried harder to find the answer to that, but I was always too afraid. Once Eliza Jane's dad and grandpa came through here, that's when I realized I had to do something. By the time I had come up with a plan, they had both died, so I had to readjust."

"And what exactly was that plan? Because I'm still not sure about it," Malbec asked.

"It was kind of simple but brilliant." His mother smiled. "And it's working." She waved her hand between the two of them. "Look at you. You're both glowing with sexual satisfaction."

"Mom. Really. You need to be quiet," Malbec said

behind gritted teeth. Sometimes being Weezer's son had its perks, and other times, it was just plain difficult and embarrassing.

"You have to understand that I don't want to give up what I've worked my entire life to give to my children." His mother pushed her coffee and apple fritter aside. "I know that what my family did was wrong. And I'm trying to make it right on some levels. I want you here at the winery, and I want you to have a small piece of it. But just like you shouldn't suffer because of the mistakes of your ancestors, neither should my kids."

Malbec had to admit, he agreed with his mom. The question became, how did that look?

"I'm content with our agreement," Eliza Jane said.

"You mean the contract that I saw yesterday?" Malbec questioned and then swallowed. That seemed too small a piece of the pie now that he knew the truth. "I think we need to go back to the drawing board on that."

"What do you mean? Why?" Eliza Jane folded her arms across her chest. "I could ask for a whole lot more."

"I think my brother is trying to give you more," Merlot said with a slight laugh. "How much more are you talking?"

"Not a lot. But she deserves more of her line after it gets off the ground, and I think if she and I aren't a couple after Mom and Dad give up their shares in the winery, she's an equal equity partner like all of us kids."

"Well, I'll be damned," his father said. "That's mighty generous of you."

"It is only fair," Malbec said.

"I have to agree." Merlot nodded. "I don't necessarily like giving up part of the winery, but based on what is being said, if our great-grandfather basically stole it, then it's the least we can do."

Malbec's mother took a napkin and dabbed at her eyes. "What makes you think you won't be a couple in a few years?" She sniffed.

His father burst out laughing. "That's what you're stuck on?"

"Of course, it is. Look at how perfect they are. I mean, he hasn't stopped touching her since we sat down. And, well, her hand is pretty high up on his thigh."

Eliza Jane jerked her hand to her lap.

Everyone at the table chuckled.

"Wait a second." Merlot waved his finger. "If they end up getting married or something, Do they own more of the winery than the rest of us?"

"Married?" Eliza Jane fanned her face. "Oh, Lord. People warned me about working for Weezer, but this was never on the agenda."

His mother leaned across the table and took her hand. "Are you going to stay on? Will you sign that contract?"

Malbec held his breath. If she stayed, he would fly back to Napa, quit his job, and pack up and come home tomorrow.

Shit.

That was about the craziest thought he'd ever had. Yet, it felt so normal.

He was absolutely becoming his mother. Or maybe his father. Or perhaps a combination of the two.

"I plan on it," Eliza Jane said.

"Malbec," his father said. "What are your plans? Are you going back to Napa Valley and leaving things to Eliza Jane here?"

"Or are you going to make this a family affair again? Because I want to come back and work more at the winery, and I know Chablis is talking with the volunteer fire department here. Riesling won't ever work for the family business, but we have three of the best wine pushers in the industry in our back pocket," Merlot said. "I think we'd make a great team."

"Do you think there is room for all of us at The River Winery?" Malbec asked.

Merlot nodded. "I can check my ego. Can you?"

"I don't know. That's asking a lot of that man." Eliza Jane reached out and ruffled his hair. "I've only spent one night with him and he's really a lot to handle."

"Sounds like it's all settled." His mother brought a napkin to her nose and blew. "Now we just have to deal with that bitch, Racheal."

"What do you think she's going to find in that book?" Eliza Jane asked.

"Unless mother put in a picture of that sign, nothing," Weezer said. "I'm not even sure she knew. My father and grandfather told me that I was to never tell Carter."

"But she told me the first night we were together. She needed to have someone on her side, and that was always me," Malbec's dad said.

"Mom, why didn't you tell Dad about how Great-grandpa cheated Eliza Jane's family out of the winery?" Merlot asked. "Is that why you divorced?"

"It was because I was worried about Eliza Jane's family ever coming back and trying to take it from us. If his name—or you all—were involved, you'd be liable somehow, and I didn't want that. So, I pushed you all away."

"That makes so much sense," Merlot said. "You just summed up so many things in one sentence." He rose and closed the gap between him and their mother. "I love you."

"I love you, too, son." Their mother gave him a big hug and kiss. "Everything I've done has been to protect my family."

"We know that," Malbec said. "We just now have to deal with Racheal and, unfortunately, I think that is a waiting game."

"Agreed," his father said. "We might as well go

about our day until we hear from Zinfandel, or until the shit hits the fan."

Malbec stood, offering his hand to Eliza Jane. "If you don't mind, Eliza Jane and I are going to play hooky."

"Go right ahead," his mother said. "Maybe Merlot can come into the winery today and help out."

"I'd love to," Merlot said. "Let's touch base this evening."

"Family dinner at my place," his father said. "Seven sharp. I'll gather the troops."

"We'll be there." Malbec stood and made his way toward his mother. He helped her to her feet. "Thank you for doing what you thought would protect us and for now telling me, and more importantly, Eliza Jane the truth."

"It was time it came out. But I really don't want Racheal to blast it out on the evening news."

"No one does," Malbec said. "But even if she does, it won't matter anymore. We have Eliza Jane on our side." He kissed his mother's cheek. "It's all working out how you wanted it."

"That it is. Now go have a good time." His mother smiled. "You know, Faith had a premonition or something about the two of you that included marriage and babies."

"I'm going to pretend I didn't hear that," Malbec said. He took Eliza Jane by the hand and led her back toward the library. "I'm sorry for the craziness that is my family."

"I'm not. I like them, even though they are putting a million carts before one horse." She waggled her finger under his nose. "I like you. And I'm willing to go on dates with you. But that's as far as this goes for now, got it?"

"As long as you don't have a problem with me moving back to Candlewood Falls."

"God, I thought you'd never make that decision."

He laughed. "What shall we do today?"

"Spend it in bed?"

"You don't have to ask me twice."

14

ELIZA JANE

Eliza Jane pulled Malbec's shirt over her head and took the tub of chocolate ice cream he offered. "I feel so guilty."

"Why?" He flopped back onto the bed and crossed his legs while he surfed the channels on the television.

"For one, I'm not sure I'll be able to walk tomorrow."

Malbec laughed. "Feel free to keep stroking my ego. Or something else if you're so inclined."

She slapped his arm. "We're done for the foreseeable future. I'd be shocked if you could even do anything after the day we've had."

"Yeah. I'm not a teenager anymore, that's for damn sure." He pointed the remote at the TV. "But, seriously, why do you have a case of the guilts? And please don't tell me you're having second thoughts about the contract or the revisions I want to make to it."

"No. It's not that," she said. "I'm worried about Merlot. I feel like he's still really hurting over this Racheal woman and what she did and what she might still do to him."

"My dad will take care of that. Besides, after talking at length with Merlot, it's nearly impossible that the baby she lost was his. The timing was off."

She twisted her body and snuggled closer to Malbec. In just one short week, she felt as if she'd found home —in more ways than one. "He really loved her."

"I believe he did, and that breaks my heart. I should have been a better brother and more attentive. But even Merlot will tell you that it's in the past. And even if she outs the way we acquired the winery, you have the power to control that narrative."

"I could really fuck you all over, even after I sign that contract, just in the way I choose to tell the story."

"But would you do that?"

"Only if you break my heart." She pressed her lips against his, but he jerked his head away.

"Fuck," he mumbled. "Racheal is about to make some kind of statement." He turned up the volume on the television.

Eliza Jane focused on the TV and bolted to an upright position. "I've met her."

"Excuse me?"

"That woman. She was at the coffee shop the first day I drove into town, and she approached me when I came out of the spa."

"Did she say anything to you?"

"I think the first time I saw her, I mentioned that I was going to be working at the winery. The second time, she came into the winery and asked if any of you were around but didn't want to talk to you. She bought some wine and a cheese plate. The third time was outside the hair salon, and she made some really weird comments."

"So, she's been hanging around town watching. Fucking bitch."

"Why wouldn't anyone say anything?"

"Her dad has cancer. And her parents are good people. No one wants to upset them. And other than us, no one knows what she might be doing. It's not like Merlot is going around telling people that it's him in that picture. He doesn't want people thinking he's actually having an affair with her when it's not true."

"I need to call him." Malbec reached for his cell. "Hey, Siri, call Merlot." He put it on speaker.

The phone rang twice.

"What's up?"

"Did you know Racheal was in town?" Malbec asked. "And just so you know, you're on speaker, and Eliza Jane can hear you."

"Hey, Eliza Jane. Is my brother treating you like a princess?"

"If that means getting ice cream in bed, then he is."

"Good. Make sure that includes some good wine," Merlot said. "Are you watching the five o'clock news?"

"I missed most of it. Why?"

"Well, she named me as the man she's having an affair with. Dad is going ballistic. He tossed a few books across the room, and Mom was ready to race down the street to Racheal's parents' house with a *loaded* shotgun."

"So should you," Eliza Jane said. "Especially since it's not true. And I think I should tell you that Racheal approached me twice since I came to town."

"Why am I not surprised?" Merlot said. "She's a piece of work."

"What I want to know is why you aren't angrier over what's happening," Eliza Jane said.

"I'm with her on this one." He pointed the remote at the television and turned up the volume more.

"Because she can't hurt me or us anymore," Merlot said. "First, I can prove I'm not the father of her baby."

"How?" Malbec asked.

"Did you listen to any of the press conference?" Merlot asked. "She made the mistake of showing the dates of her hospital stay. That was three months after she and I were together."

"How can you prove that?" Eliza Jane asked. "No offense. But that's just your word against hers."

"Because after she dumped me, I went to Europe," Merlot said. "I was gone for two months, and that would mean she would have been about five months pregnant when she lost the baby."

"Oh," Eliza Jane said. "According to her interview, she was only two months."

"Yeah. She didn't think that through very well, and my dad is going to enjoy making this a legal nightmare for her," Merlot said. "And it gets better."

"How so?" Malbec leaned back on the pillows and crossed his legs. "God, I wish we were all together with a big bowl of popcorn."

"If it's any consolation, Mom made some, and Zinfandel and I are enjoying it while Dad drafts legal papers. He's in his freaking glory, though he does feel bad for her parents for what he's about to do to her."

"Well, she deserves it," Malbec said. "I didn't get to see most of the announcement. What did she say about the winery?"

"Nothing," Merlot said. "She couldn't find anything in that history book, so she just came after me. And she failed."

"I'm sorry she dragged your good name through—"

"Shut up, big brother," Merlot said. "Are you home to stay?"

Malbec turned his head and caught Eliza Jane's gaze.

She smiled. Her heart hammered in her chest as she nodded.

"I am," he said.

"Then this little blip on the radar was worth it. I guess I'd better turn in my notice and plan on working full-time at the winery. Does that work for you?"

Eliza Jane reached across the bed and lifted the phone in her hand. "Only if you're willing to take orders from me."

"Oh. That could be fun," Merlot said.

"Hey, that's my girlfriend you're talking to," Malbec said. "I won't have you flirting with Eliza Jane."

"Are you jealous, big brother?"

"Damn fucking straight, I am," Malbec said.

Eliza Jane handed him the cell. "I think I'm going to like being a part of the winery and this family."

"We've only been together a week, and you already think you're family?" Malbec tapped the screen, hanging up on his brother. "Next thing I know, you're going to want to move in here with me."

She gasped. "What are you talking about? I already live here."

"Where do you expect me to live then?"

"Hell if I know." She wrapped her arms around his shoulders. "But if you're really nice to me, I'll let you stay for a few weeks or months while we figure things out."

"Oh, gee. Thanks."

"You're welcome." She rested her head on his chest. She had no idea what the future had in store for them. She'd taken a big risk by moving to Candlewood Falls, and an even bigger one by letting Malbec River into her heart.

But something told her that this was a risk worth taking. That her life had taken a turn for the better the moment she'd agreed to work for Weezer River. It didn't matter what their families had done in the past or the betrayals that both great-grandfathers had left as a legacy for their families.

She and Malbec had a chance to right both wrongs.

And not only were they committed to doing exactly that—

So was his family.

Right there on the river's edge, she'd get her chance to make her father proud, and Malbec would be able to carry on three generations of great wine.

It was a union that was meant to be.

"Do you ever think we'll be able to figure out how your great-grandfather cheated at that poker game?" She lifted her gaze. "Your mom said there are other secrets buried on this property."

"Ah, the box of secrets. Yes. My grandfather thought the old doctor buried a box somewhere by his office."

"Office? Where?" she asked.

"Yeah, the building we use for overflow now. We used to rent it to a local doctor for his private practice until about thirty-ish years ago."

"He used it as an exam room? It's kind of small."

"No. He used it for his adoption agency. He helped a lot of women who couldn't have children find mothers who couldn't, for whatever reason, keep their babies. He was pretty revered in this town."

"What happened to him?"

"He retired and moved south about thirty-five or so years ago, and we decided we needed the space back."

"That's kind of a sweet story. I'm glad our winery did something like that. I mean bringing families together is a big deal."

"My mom always enjoyed seeing babies placed in good homes. She's a big softy when you get to know her."

"I wish someone would tell me how she got the name Weezer."

"You and me both." He laughed. "I will never admit this in front of my mother, but I think she was right."

"About what?"

"You."

Eliza Jane smiled. "You mean because I'm such an awesome winemaker, and you'd be so lost without me in the winery?"

"You've got the I'd-be-lost-without-you part right." He kissed her nose. "I have no idea what the future holds, but I want to see what we can make of it. Together."

She closed her eyes and let her body relax into his loving embrace. It was crazy to feel so much in such a short time. Or to trust so easily. However, her heart knew that this was exactly where she belonged. "I have a feeling this is going to be the start of a very long partnership."

EPILOGUE
MALBEC

Halloween

"Where are you taking me?"

Malbec kept his hands over Eliza Jane's eyes as he guided her down the path toward the river's edge and the dock where'd they'd shared many romantic lunches.

The last two months had been the best of his life. He couldn't imagine a life without Eliza Jane in it.

"Okay. You can open your eyes now." He dropped his hands and took a step back.

His parents and Merlot had helped him set up two chairs and a table, along with a feast that included his father's fried chicken, his mother's macaroni and cheese, and a bottle of pinot noir.

And, of course, a few cannolis for dessert—but that would be for after the big question.

If Malbec ever got up the courage to ask.

Lately, he'd had this horrible problem where his tongue got all tied up when he was around the woman he loved more than life itself.

"Oh, my God. This is amazing." She did a little dance as she brought her hands to her cheeks. "What's the occasion?"

"It's Halloween."

She tilted her head and glared. "That's not a reason to have a picnic by the river's edge."

"It is in Candlewood Falls. Didn't you know it's a tradition around these parts?" He pulled back the folding chair and waved his hand.

"You're funny." She sat and took a sip of wine. "Now, tell me what's really going on."

"Can't a guy show his girl a little love on a special night?"

"Halloween is about scaring the shit out of each other. I think you're confusing this with Valentine's Day." She raised her glass. "But whatever. I'm happy to have a nice dinner, especially when it's your parents' cooking."

"Are you saying mine sucks?"

"Yes. Unless it's steaks on the grill."

He laughed, holding up his glass. "Cheers to us."

"I can clink my glass to that."

He took a long sip before setting his beverage down on the table. He cleared his throat. "Are you happy?"

She cocked her head. "What kind of question is that?"

"Just answer it."

"Of course, I am."

"Do you love me?"

"You're being weird," she said. "Yes. I love you. Do you love me back?"

He chuckled. "I love you so much it hurts." He stood and dug into his pocket. It was now or never. "I never want to know what life looks like without you in it."

"Oh, shit. You're not going to do this now, are you?"

"Do what?"

"Propose," she whispered. "Oh. God. I'm going to ruin it. I suck at life."

He laughed. "No. You make life worth living." He pulled out the ring box and set it on the table. He decided not to get down on one knee. Eliza Jane was a lot of things, but traditional wasn't one of them. He flipped open the lid, showing off his mother's engagement ring. Weezer had wanted him to have it sooner rather than later. "I love you. I don't want to wait to get married. I want to do it now. As in as soon as possible."

"Like next weekend?" She lifted the ring out of the box and held it up in the air. "Holy shit. This is your mom's."

"She wants you to have it."

Eliza Jane pressed one hand against her heart. "I don't know if I can accept this."

"You will insult her if you agree to marry me and don't take that ring."

"Talk about fucking pressure." She inhaled sharply and sighed. "Wow," she whispered. "I love you. And, yes, I want to marry you. With all my heart, I want to be with you forever."

He helped her slip the ring onto her finger.

It was a perfect fit.

A loud, thunderous clapping roared in the background.

She turned and let out a gasp as his entire family emerged. "Are you kidding me right now?"

"Did you think I could get engaged and not have them present?" He stood and held out his hand.

She took it, and he lifted her into his arms. "I hope someone got that on video."

"Oh, yeah," one of his siblings said.

She rested her head on Malbec's shoulder.

Finally, she'd come home.

Thank you for taking the time to read *Rivers Edge*. I hope you enjoyed your stay in Candlewood Falls. Please feel free to leave an honest review. Next in the series is: **The Buried Secret.** And please check out the rest of the series:

Its In His Kiss

Lips Of An Angel
Kisses Sweeter than Wine
A Little Bit Whiskey

Grab a glass of vino, kick back, relax, and let the romance roll in…

Sign up for my Newsletter (https://dl.bookfunnel.com/82gm8b9k4y) where I often give away free books before publication.

Join my private Facebook group (https://www.facebook.com/groups/191706547909047/) where I post exclusive excerpts and discuss all things murder and love!

READY FOR ANOTHER TRIP TO CANDLEWOOD FALLS?

For more Alpachino the Alpaca antics and to find out who went to prison for killing Sam's Father's read <u>TAKING ROOT</u> by Stacey Wilk.

And the second book in Stacey's series…What will Brad Wilde the man who has it all do when an orphan is dropped on his doorstep? RAISING WINTER by Stacey Wilk.

Also by Stacey Wilk in this series: Even the most unexpected circumstances may teach us how to forgive what cannot be changed. DEFINING CHANCES.

And While packing away her mothers life, Petra Wilde discovers a life of her own in BEGINNING OVER.

If you want to spend some time with Sam Wilde and his quest for an apple to make you happy and horny you'll want to read WILDE TEMPTATION by K.M. FAWCETT.

And the second book in K.M. Fawcett's series…Spend the holidays with Lacey Wilde, her dog Remi, and a sexy marine who claims Remi belongs to him in <u>WILDE CHRISTMAS</u> by K.M. Fawcett.

Also by K.M. Fawcett is WILD IN LOVE: Can a bad boy and a
good girl overcome their fears to find true love?

And in WILDE TREASURES: While searching for a hidden
fortune, can two lonely adventurers discover some treasurers
are more precious than gold.

ACKNOWLEDGMENTS

A big thank you to Stacey Wilk and K.M. Fawcett for inviting me into Candlewood Falls.

ABOUT THE AUTHOR

Jen Talty is the *USA Today* Bestselling Author of Contemporary Romance, Romantic Suspense, and Paranormal Romance. In the fall of 2020, her short story was selected and featured in a 1001 Dark Nights Anthology.

Regardless of the genre, her goal is to take you on a ride that will leave you floating under the sun with warmth in your heart. She writes stories about broken heroes and heroines who aren't necessarily looking for romance, but in the end, they find the kind of love books are written about :).

She first started writing while carting her kids to one hockey rink after the other, averaging 170 games per year between 3 kids in 2 countries and 5 states. Her first book, IN TWO WEEKS was originally published in 2007. In 2010 she helped form a publishing company (Cool Gus Publishing) with *NY Times* Bestselling Author Bob Mayer where she ran the technical side of the business through 2016.

Jen is currently enjoying the next phase of her life...the empty nester! She and her husband reside in Jupiter, Florida.

Grab a glass of vino, kick back, relax, and let the romance roll in...

Sign up for my *Newsletter (https://dl.bookfunnel.com/82gm8b9k4y)* where I often give away free books before publication.

Join my private *Facebook group* (https://www.facebook.com/groups/191706547909047/) where I post exclusive excerpts and discuss all things murder and love!

Never miss a new release. Follow me on Amazon:amazon.com/author/jentalty

And on Bookbub: bookbub.com/authors/jen-talty

ALSO BY JEN TALTY

Everyone needs a SAFE HARBOR!

Mine To Keep

Mine To Save

Mine To Protect

Mine to Hold

Mine to Love

Check out LOVE IN THE ADIRONDACKS!

Shattered Dreams

An Inconvenient Flame

The Wedding Driver

Clear Blue Sky

Blue Moon

Before the Storm

NY STATE TROOPER SERIES (also set in the Adirondacks!)

In Two Weeks

Dark Water

Deadly Secrets

Murder in Paradise Bay

To Protect His own

Deadly Seduction

When A Stranger Calls

His Deadly Past

The Corkscrew Killer

First Responders: A spin-off from the NY State Troopers series

Playing With Fire

Private Conversation

The Right Groom

After The Fire

Caught In The Flames

Chasing The Fire

Legacy Series

Dark Legacy

Legacy of Lies

Secret Legacy

Emerald City

Investigate Away

Sail Away

Fly Away

Flirt Away

Hawaii Brotherhood Protectors

Waylen Unleashed

Whiskey Sour

Whiskey Cobbler

Whiskey Smash

Irish Whiskey

The Monroes

Color Me Yours

Color Me Smart

Color Me Free

Color Me Lucky

Color Me Ice

Color Me Home

Search and Rescue

Protecting Ainsley

Protecting Clover

Protecting Olympia

Protecting Freedom

Protecting Princess

Protecting Marlowe

Fallport Rescue Operations

Searching for Madison

Searching for Haven

Searching for Pandora

Searching for Stormi

DELTA FORCE-NEXT GENERATION

Shielding Jolene

Shielding Aalyiah

Shielding Laine

Shielding Talullah

Shielding Maribel

Shielding Daisy

The Men of Thief Lake

Rekindled

Destiny's Dream

Federal Investigators

Jane Doe's Return

The Butterfly Murders

THE AEGIS NETWORK

The Sarich Brother

The Lighthouse

Her Last Hope

The Last Flight

The Return Home

The Matriarch

Aegis Network: Jacksonville Division

A SEAL's Honor

Talon's Honor

Arthur's Honor

Rex's Honor

Kent's Honor

Buddy's Honor

Aegis Network Short Stories

Max & Milian

A Christmas Miracle

Spinning Wheels

Holiday's Vacation

The Brotherhood Protectors

Out of the Wild

Rough Justice

Rough Around The Edges

Rough Ride

Rough Edge

Rough Beauty

The Brotherhood Protectors

The Saving Series

Saving Love

Saving Magnolia

Saving Leather

Hot Hunks

Cove's Blind Date Blows Up

My Everyday Hero – Ledger

Tempting Tavor

Malachi's Mystic Assignment

Needing Neor

Holiday Romances

A Christmas Getaway

Alaskan Christmas

Whispers

Christmas In The Sand

Heroes & Heroines on the Field

Taking A Risk

Tee Time

A New Dawn

The Blind Date

Spring Fling

Summers Gone

Winter Wedding

The Awakening

Fated Moons

The Collective Order

The Lost Sister

The Lost Soldier

The Lost Soul

The Lost Connection

The New Order

www.ingramcontent.com/pod-product-compliance
Lightning Source LLC
Chambersburg PA
CBHW010737130726
47899CB00015B/3303